I0548938

1

Walker Between the Worlds

Book 1 of the Sibyl Chronicles

Marlene Pardo Pellicer

No parts of this book may be reproduced by any mechanical, photographic or electronic process or in the form of a phonographic recording; nor may it be stored in a retrieval system, transmitted or otherwise copied for public or private use other than as brief quotations embodied in articles and reviews, without prior written permission from the author.

WALKER BETWEEN THE WORLDS: BOOK 1 OF THE SIBYL CHRONICLES. Copyright © Marlene Pardo Pellicer. First Printing 2019. Printed in the United States of America

This book is a work of fiction. Any references to historical events, real people or real places are used fictitiously. Other names, characters, places and events are products of the author's imagination and any resemblance to actual events or places or persons, living or dead is entirely coincidental.

First Edition:
First Printing

PUBLISHED BY ELEVENTH HOUR LLC
www.11thhour.company

E-BOOK ISBN 978-0-9991605-6-5
PRINT ISBN 978-0-9991605-7-2

I dedicate this book to Giovanni, Elizabeth and Luca the most beloved of those I love.

———————————————

Special thanks to Brandon Calvet for his ideas on new demons such as the Trezor Underling and the Kyoki Soldier Demon.

———————————————

A petit homage to Manly Wade Wellman and his short story *The Horror Undying*.

About The Author

Marlene has been in love with writing since she was eleven years old; but as they say better late than never.
She is a native Miamian and the founder of Miami Ghost Chronicles. She has been a paranormal researcher since the 1990s and is the producer and host of *Stories of the Supernatural*. She is also the narrator of the podcast show *Nightshade Diary, Supernatural StoryTime* and the blog author of *Stranger Than Fiction Stories*.
Marlene lives with her husband Henry on a micro-farm in Miami's 100-year-old agricultural belt, surrounded by several dogs, exotic birds, chickens and a rescue rabbit named Thelma.

www.MarlenePardo.com

Other Books by Marlene

Haunted History of the Old West's Wicked Ladies & The Bad Hombres They Loved (2017)
The Lady in the Blue Kimono: Film Noir Murders (2018)
Supernatural Safety: A Paranormal DIY Guide (2018)

Table of Content

PROLOGUE

Night pressed against windows, and children slept huddled under thick blankets with a nightlight nearby. Their parents cradled a hot drink as they binged on their favorite TV show. They felt safe behind their locked doors.

In a place that could have been on a different planet, the late hour welcomed those who flourished in shadows. An icy wind slivered between abandoned buildings that stood like dispassionate sentinels. A few cars lined the deserted street, smoke curling from the exhaust as they idled to keep the heater inside running. Steamed-up windows hid the occupants from sight who were there for one reason only; they were johns or pimps.

A man who neither sought safety nor provided it, inhaled deeply as saliva squirted into his mouth. It took all his willpower to push down on the accelerator and keep his truck traveling at a slow, but steady speed down the street. His eyes were avaricious portals, feasting on his unfulfilled fantasy standing alone under the dim light of a flickering street lamp. In that moment, he dubbed her "Fantasy Girl".

The girl's eyes were large and liquid, accentuated by blonde pigtails that jiggled in the wind cheerleader-like. The man guessed her age to be no more than fifteen. She wore a lime green parka, dark jeans and black boots. Her gloved hand gripped the pole of the lamp as if she feared being swept away. He knew the script, money gone, no place to sleep, no food to eat. Why else would she be standing on a street corner in such a godforsaken part of town?

The man saw desperation etched on her face. Vulnerable and alone, her expression added to the precarious position she held this night. In a sordid world, which saw her as nothing more than fresh meat, her allure lassoed him securely and he knew he could not leave without her. The predators were circling, including him.

The other working girls had staked out their turf two blocks away, leaving those they rejected to slither down the lonely boulevard to where she stood.

In the time, it took him to circle around he made his plans. He envisioned every moment that Fantasy Girl would be his captive. The ending unknown, but he anticipated it would be deeply satisfying.

His faded pick-up turned the corner of where she stood, and he saw a dark vehicle pulled up next to her. Her grip on the pole had not relaxed, and she shook her head. Whoever sat inside the car said something to her that made her draw back. She shook her head again. The anonymous car swung back into the street with an angry squeal of rubber.

He drew on all his prior experience, rehearsing in his mind how to say the right thing, the right way to gain her trust, and get her inside next to him, only an arm's reach away. His rust bucket pulled up next to her, and he reached over to roll down his passenger side window. He fixed his most disarming and open smile on his face.

"Hey, my name is Slim, are you okay?"

She eyed him with distrust, looking into the semi-darkness of the interior as she spoke, "Yeah, kinda."

"Look before you get the wrong idea, I'm not a john or a pimp..."

She cut him off, "Are you a cop?"

"No, not that either. I know you're new in town, because I work for St. Mary Magdalene's Church, and I come down here to help anyone who needs a place to sleep, or some food to eat. I can offer you a ride, no questions asked."

The thin man then stayed quiet, watching her face as despair warred with caution. He pulled down the visor and produced a battered, laminated identification card. His picture on the front showed the same smile, above the name Sam Loveless, and a non-descript title from the church's outreach program. He gave it to her. This made-up badge served to lure many a victim into his clutches.

He used his toothy smile again. "Even if you don't go with me, my advice is to leave and go home. It's dangerous out here. Do you want the address? You can go there tomorrow, but it's pretty far."

She looked at the ID card, and then handed it back to him. "How far is it?"

"It's across town, a few miles from here. That's why they send me, Slim's Chauffer Service, it's not a limo but it'll do." He made his eyes twinkle, but her face remained set and withdrawn. "Well, at least you know where to go. Hey, no pressure, just be safe."

He slid back, and used one of his best tactics. He put the truck in drive, nodded and smiled at her, then waved and looked in his rearview mirror appearing to check traffic before turning back into the street.

Her hand shot out, and gripped the door halting the truck's progress. She jerked up the manual lock and slid in, staying as far away from him as possible. The girl eyed him up and down as he sped up the truck into cruising speed.

"Why don't you roll up the window? It's cold." he said in his nicest voice.

She pulled on the handle, and the piece of glass screeched as it reached the top of the frame. The first raindrops lashed the windshield, and he turned on the wipers and smiled at her again.

"Not a moment too soon, this is a rotten night to be outdoors."

Fantasy Girl looked at him with wary eyes. He stayed quiet, thinking of which room in his cabin he would take her. Perhaps outside to the shed, the walls and floor, once splattered with blood, urine and gore were spotless once he took a brush with bleach to them. He spent the whole day on

11

that task. Fresh curtains hung in the window. A bedspread decorated with yellow flowers gave it a homey feeling. Something excited him about starting to work on a victim in that innocuous setting. He thought this is how an artist feels when standing in front of a blank canvas.

The silence yawned between them. He knew better than to ask her name.

She said suddenly, "Hey, can you do me a favor?"

"Sure."

"I need to pick up my stuff."

He nodded, "Where to?"

"It's that place down by the railroad tracks; name of Shamrock Motel. I'm only paid up till tomorrow morning, and I don't want them to keep my shit."

"I think I know which one you're talking about."

Conversation lagged between them as they left the city behind, and the landscape became lonelier and darker. Streetlights no longer lined the road, and they saw only a solitary porch light sneaking through the green darkness of the trees. Like twin lighthouses, the headlights parted the rainy gloom that swallowed the vehicle as it wound its way through the solitary back roads.

The truck squeaked as it crossed the railroad tracks, and then turned into the parking lot of a small, one story motel. It sat surrounded by tall firs that soughed in the icy wind. A lopsided, wooden sign with the hotel's name clacked against the post that anchored it. During the 1950s, it catered to the hunting crowd. Now it stood with grimy windows and peeling paint, like a forgotten mistress that has served her purpose. There were no other vehicles except for an ancient VW Beetle by the office. She pointed him to a door at the far end of the building.

"I'll be a minute."

"No hurry, take your time," he assured her. The wipers made a dull thumping as they swiped across the windshield, and his eyes followed her as she made her way to the door with a number 11 on it. She fumbled with a key and then let herself in. A light switched on, and he saw her moving about inside.

Perfect he thought, the manager would think she left before being kicked out; another nameless throwaway, whose face would soon be forgotten. Excitement coursed through his body and for a moment, he considered killing her inside the room. Just as quickly as it came, he dismissed it. Why should he cheat himself of so much pleasure through impatience?

Sudden darkness replaced the illumination inside the room. Fantasy Girl popped her head out of the door. "Hey Slim, the lights just cut out in the entire room," she called out. "Do you have a flashlight or something? I can't see where I'm going in here."

"Sure, I'll be right there."

Slim, reached into his glove compartment, and pulled out a dollar store flashlight. He then retrieved a long bowie knife with a serrated edge still in its sheath. He clipped it to the outside of his boot. The wiry man did not assume no other person waited in the room.

He turned the truck off. Icy droplets slashed down on his head as he ran the short distance to the door. It stood ajar, and he pushed it open with one hand.

From across the darkened room he recognized her voice sounding young and frightened, "Slim thanks. Almost everything is packed, but I think I got a pair of shoes under the bed."

Slim wiped rain from his face, and closed the door behind him. With the other hand, he switched on the flashlight aiming the weak stream of light to where the bed would be. The beam found an empty space with messy covers, and an open box of cookies next to the pillow. This small room did not offer much cover for an ambush. He brought his tension down a notch as he found no immediate danger.

"Hey, I haven't gotten your name."

"It's Fantasy Girl." A gravel-like, metallic voice answered him from across the room. Slim aimed the flashlight to where an outline darkened the gloom a few feet away, and it took him a few moments to realize the answer she gave to his question.

Then in a split second, all his instincts as a predator sent alarm bells off in his head. The pines overheard rustled and whistled in the night air, accentuating the silence in the room. Fear prickled along his spine, twisting his gut.

Samuel Loveless Greer saw himself standing in the darkened motel room as if watching from outside his body. He saw a wiry man with sandy hair, his face creased by working outdoors in the sun and wind for years. He looked ordinary in his frayed jeans and jacket. Thousands looked like him. Slim always made sure that his description would fit many men. The hand holding the flashlight shook. He recognized only one thing; his life depended on escaping from this place. In the blink of an eye, he found himself back inside his body, and he stepped towards the door.

His hand fumbled as he searched for the knob behind his back. A part of his brain urged him to pull out the bowie knife, but he would have to either give up the search for the exit, or keep the flashlight aimed across the room. The figure remained motionless. His hand crept down to the knife, the beam of light bouncing as his hand jerked with fear. Then he bumped into someone behind him, and his mind did not understand how anyone could creep in through a closed door. Before he could turn around, a heavy hand gripped him by the shoulder and held him in place.

A breath whispered against his ear, and a voice that sounded like a growl said, "Going somewhere, Slim?"

His dry tongue stuck to the top of his palate. He didn't even have enough spit to swallow. Figures swirled in the darkness at the edge of the room and his brain tried to make sense of it, like a child with a Rubik's Cube. How could a small motel room contain so many people?

Then from far off, he discerned a noise. The volume increased, and he realized they were voices, but they sounded inhuman. Some hissed, others growled, their words unintelligible, except there were some he understood. "He is mine, I will be first." a guttural voice rose above the others.

"No," another voice screeched, "it has been too long since I've tasted the warmth of blood in my mouth and hands."

Whatever surrounded him squabbled in grunts. They described the obscenities they wanted to inflict on him. Hot urine poured down his pant leg, when they discussed how to keep him alive so they could all have their turn.

The air inside the room became fetid with a reek worse than any charnel house ever created by him. His eyes watered and his nose twitched with the overpowering stink.

The figures grew silent and still. From across the room he saw a figure step forward, illuminated in a golden light. She, but not she; a woman dressed in her same clothing, the green parka, the dark jeans molding the long legs and the black boots, stood and looked at him steadily. He gazed at her face, and he saw she resembled the young runaway that beguiled him an hour ago. Crazy thoughts chased each other in his brain. Could this be a mother pimping out her own daughter?

The woman pursed her lips, and whistled softly. Torches came to life at the corners of the room, which expanded to dimensions that vanished into the swirling mists. The firelight then revealed what lay hidden in the frothing blackness. Slim recognized some of them as human. Others stood on four legs, a head, the only thing human still left. Most displayed fangs and curved talons for fingernails. Their eyes glimmered red or yellow as they eyed him with an insatiable hunger. However, none of them dared look at the woman, and as she stepped forward, they scurried out of her way.

Rough hands dragged Slim to the bed, tying him spread-eagled across it. The first scream escaped him, but he stopped when a creature with green scaly skin clapped in glee, and cavorted next to him each time he yelled in fear. With its long nails it scraped every bit of clothing off leaving long, bloody welts across his body.

The creature dipped a fingernail in a small pool of blood on his belly, and brought it to its mouth. "Sweet, but salty," the thing mumbled rapturously as it sucked on its finger.

Slim looked at the woman with pleading eyes, "Why are you doing this? You don't have to do this. Why?"

The red-haired woman stepped forward, and the creatures retreated into the furthest corners of the darkness.

Her voice sounded husky when she answered him, "Some dark being that crept into your soul many years ago, gave you cunning to avoid capture, and falling prey to your own stupidity. You probably would have died of old age, taking your secrets to the grave, leaving a trail of destruction and heartbreak in your wake. All done in an effort to feed the master you serve. That thing finds satisfaction only with pain and agony. Like all these that are here to feast on you. To give you in equal measure, what you meted out to your poor victims."

Slim thrashed about on the bed, and in his mind, he replayed all the scenes of depravities he committed against his victims. He understood too well, what she said; anguish not death satiated the unending appetite inside him. He developed techniques to keep his victims alive as long as possible, in order to enjoy their suffering. Criminal profilers would have classified him as a sexual sadist.

"Slim, today is your lucky day," the woman said, "welcome to purgatory."

She stepped towards the door, and the circle of creatures closed in around the bed. They still growled and snapped at each other like a pack of wolves. Some with long, gray tongues licked their putrid lips with anticipation.

The thing with green skin crouched over him, and through the space between their bodies, the woman saw when it plucked out one of his eyes with her nail, and ate it in a slow, measured fashion. That is when his scream rang out, because he understood it would be a long time before it would stop. This is what he did to his first victim, a girl in high school named Jeanine. He lured her to an abandoned house on the outskirts of town, where he knew her screaming could not be heard.

Like a sumptuous feast laid out before a starving mob, they screamed, snorted and growled urging what they should do next to the serial killer who called himself Slim.

The woman stood against the door, and then peered into the darkness behind the creatures. She saw two figures, human figures. They did not take part in the orgy of blood. They hung their heads, and one turned towards the wall unable to see the violence being done to the man who screamed in a high-pitched voice.

These were ready; they were cleansed in purgatory, and Evil existed outside of their souls. The demons that once demanded their obedience and subservience to be paid in blood were removed. They found no joy in destroying another human being; they did not relish seeing a living thing suffer. Their bloodlust ended.

She beckoned the woman and man to follow, and she opened the door and led them outside. The rain had stopped, but moisture still clung in the air. The sounds from the room were silenced when she closed the door, and innocent lamplight filtered through the curtains.

The Elizabethan woman wore a russet red gown. A stiff ruff collar encircled her neck, and a snood stitched with pearls caught her hair. The man's garb consisted of the simple robes of a monk. He lived during the times of the Crusades.

The pair stared at the tall woman with wondering eyes. She remembered them both, since she brought them to purgatory hundreds of years before. Ema realized that she looked different now. She became for a moment in time, what they envisioned their perfect victim to be, in a guise irresistible to them. The Elizabethan woman saw a young maiden, the monk, a boy with curly hair and sad eyes.

She pointed towards the forest behind them. Two pearls of light lengthened in the indigo darkness. Her voice sounded kind, when she said, "You are both free."

Each one walked towards a luminescent opening. A sweet, rose scent filled the area, and it lingered a few moments as the figures dissolved into the light and it winked out.

The woman climbed into the old pickup truck. The keys were in the ignition; no doubt, Slim anticipated the need for a quick getaway. She backed the vehicle out, and the crunch of the tires on the gravel made a lonely sound as she turned onto the road. An early November gale swayed the truck as it retraced its route back to town.

The pickup once abandoned would be hauled away after a few days. Worthless, the tow yard expected the owner on record would never come for it. It would end up as scrap metal.

As to Slim, no trace of him would be found. FBI investigators would swarm the property once the truth became evident of the house of horrors he had created. The most elusive mystery would be the fate of the killer. He now resided as one of those who existed in purgatory hounded by a hunger that would find no appeasement... until one day.

The motel room messy and in disarray, held nothing to arouse suspicion of anything unusual having taken place. If anyone ever sprayed Luminol that would be a different story, even those creatures did not lick every drop of blood away. It wouldn't be the first time a homicide investigation discovered evidence of a previous murder.

The truck bumped over the railroad tracks, and she made her way to the older part of the town. Victorian mansions that once housed the affluent lined the deserted streets. The run-down houses with sagging porches, and overgrown yards were long ago converted to apartments.

She pulled down a lonely street next to a deserted factory, and parked the truck. She would walk a few blocks to where her human lay sleeping. This living cocoon housed her between the times the damned were brought to purgatory. Her timing when claiming this last person could have been better. When she left the body, it kept on breathing and functioning to stay alive, but the animus inside of it had flown. Sometimes this proved to be convenient, but as she saw the glow of a fire toward where she lived, she dreaded what she would find.

A fire truck barreled down the street she walked on, sirens and lights at full blast. She rounded the corner and saw the old, wooden mansion engulfed in flames. Her human lived on the top floor, and she saw the occupants of the two other apartments standing outside. They were hustled away by the paramedics. One of them kept babbling to a fireman about the girl that lived on the third floor.

The fire popped and hissed as firemen doused it with water, and sparks flew into the air when the main staircase crumbled into the circle of flames.

The redheaded woman named Ema stood staring at the conflagration. She recognized without a doubt that her avatar's body, left in the bed had burned to a crisp. In this moment, she needed to keep a level head. She faced two immediate problems; one, to locate another human on the brink of death that she could take over. Identifying the enemy who robbed her of a living pocket though, outweighed all other needs. Accidents were rare in her world, and coincidences even more so. God knew she had cultivated enough foes, in and out of hell, through hundreds of years that could have a hand in this.

I. The Little Death

TEXAS, 1851. Fort Phantom Hill sat on a lonely, barren stretch of land long inhabited by the fierce Comanche tribe, earning the area the name of Comancheria. It formed part of a chain of forts that sat on the western frontier. Soldiers would patrol a route often used by those trekking out west through Texas, then onto California after the discovery of gold in 1849.

Comanche, Lipan, Wichita, Kiowa and Kickapoo visited the outpost, but the encounters were always peaceful. The commander at the fort never understood why a sentry shot at what he described as an Indian on a nearby hill.

The morning sun shone overhead when the soldiers rode out into the arid landscape, but found nothing. A grove of blackjack oaks grew nearby. The ground lay undisturbed, absent of any evidence that anyone had been there.

The sentry named Wellman suffered teasing about shooting at a ghost in silence. He smiled and grimaced taking the comments in stride, however he had no doubt he saw someone looking towards the fort. He thought of the story told by a group of settlers and miners heading out west only a few days before.

They were a strange lot, most of them men. One stood out, even though at first glance he appeared unassuming. A young man with pale fuzz covering his upper lip, and baby fat softening the edge of his jaw sat quietly among the group. Colorless lashes fringed his sky-blue eyes.

He remembered thinking the boy looked too young to be traveling alone, until a moment when their eyes met across the campfire. Then he saw something that almost made him drop his tin cup filled with coffee. The blue eyes turned a dark green color, like storm clouds. In that moment, a certainty filled him that someone hard and infinitely older stared back at hm. Then the boy looked down and when he raised his eyes, they were the same limpid pools of blue.

Private Wellman excused himself, and stepped back from the dancing flames where the group gathered around the fire. A slight chill replaced the desert heat, and the dark bowl of the night twinkled in a cloudless sky overhead.

He listened to their conversation from the shifting murkiness beyond the light of the glowing embers, perplexed as to what he witnessed a few moments before. Then the boy who called himself Morti Peccatum, started to tell a story, and all fell silent. Only the crackle of the fire and the howl of a lone coyote competed with his voice.

They'd stopped at a fort on the way west where two sentries were murdered. The pink light of dawn crested the horizon when they found the first body. Someone had butchered it, cutting away the fleshiest parts. The following day another soldier lay mutilated in the same fashion. Indian raiders were blamed, and a scouting party headed out from the fort.

Once upon the prairie they caught a band of Comanche unaware, and captured the ones unable to flee on their ponies. The Comanche denied killing the sentries, and told of their pursuit of what they called a devil who stalked children and women from the darkness outside their campfires. Even warriors fell prey to the devil. They said this creature lurked among the white men.

The soldiers did not believe the story, and took the prisoners back with them to the fort. The Comanche feared entering the stronghold, and the commander perplexed by their reaction ordered they should be held in the hospital building. One of the Indians disappeared the following morning. The soldiers did not understand how despite being wounded and well guarded, he escaped. The dawn of their second day of captivity found another Comanche missing.

The commander called Sergeant Stanlas to come before him, and make a full report of the incident. The Comanche warriors who were known for their fierceness, wailed in fear when they saw the sergeant. They said that this is the "devil of the fort" who carried away their two other companions.

Stanlas denied the charge, pulled out his saber, and slashed at the face of the warrior accusing him. They placed him under arrest, and searched his one-room cabin. Loose floorboards were pulled up, and the soldiers gathered around in horror to stare at the flayed corpses of both Comanche, lying in a shallow grave.

The sergeant stood quiet for a time when confronted with the grisly evidence, and then he confessed to murdering and eating both men. He called himself a cannibal. He described how he killed, butchered and ate the dead sentries. However, these were only his latest victims. When he lived in the East, he cannibalized many men, women and children. He lost count of how many. The soldier taking notes of the confession gagged as Stanlas described his hunger for human flesh, and his predilection for the heart and liver.

The court-martial resulted in a verdict of guilty. The sergeant told the commander he had a last request. He wanted to be burned alive. The officers saw this as further evidence of his sick mind, and decided instead to execute him by firing squad.

Many soldiers volunteered to carry out the execution. The sergeant in charge of the detail inspected the bullet-riddled corpse. He stumbled backwards when Stanlas' eyelids quivered, and then opened. He drew his pistol and shot the man point-blank in the head. The medical officer then pronounced him dead. The sun set over a turquoise sky, when a detail buried the body far from the regular cemetery. They recited no prayers, or erected a marker over the grave.

Private Wellman recalled the details of the story, as he mounted his horse to ride back to the fort. He held the truth of what he saw in a dark corner of his mind, to be examined closer when he lived far from this place. He told neither the sergeant, nor the commander what he saw in the first light of dawn. It had simply been a man in a cavalry uniform with side-striped pantaloons, and a dragoon jacket with three, sergeant chevrons on the sleeve. Startled, he stared at the apparition, but then it turned to stare at him, and from under the round, visored cap he saw its eyes glimmered like those of an   animal.

II. Dark Appetites

LARAMIE, WYOMING TERRITORY, 1879. Mort Peccatum hunched his broad shoulders as he turned up the collar of his black duster, and pulled down the brim of his low-crowned hat against a constant drizzle that swept through the platform of the Laramie train depot. Snow lingered on the tall peaks surrounding the town, perhaps into late summer.

Most of the passengers disembarked. Only those waiting for heavy luggage or animals, stood impatiently under the rain. He heard his horse Zabuca whinny upon smelling his scent when he approached the ramp. The freight door opened. A bay mare with a long black tail and mane emerged; he motioned for the reins and walked the horse down.

The rain increased, and it drew a sullen veil across the fading light, cooling the temperatures of the July afternoon. Squinting from under his dripping hat brim, he waved to a man sitting on a buckboard. The old cowboy slapped the reins, and the horse pulled the wagon to where Mort stood. He tied Zabuca securely to the back, and then threw his saddle and other luggage into the wagon, which he covered with an oilskin blanket. He climbed in next to the driver, holding in one hand a leather scabbard that held his Winchester rifle.

Mort sat in silence as they pulled away from the depot area. The Union Pacific locomotive emitted a loud whistle to alert that it would be leaving soon. The horses' hooves, muffled by the muddy road, made slurping sounds as they headed towards Laramie's main street. Contrary to appearances, Mort studied everything around him, assessing if there were any risks beforehand. He understood that only the foolhardy took unnecessary chances. The reality of his existence pivoted around survival. Underneath his coat, a Colt six-shooter hung low on his belt.

Well-built businesses and homes lined neat streets, in place of the ramshackle buildings and tents of the first years of the town. The hell-roaring, mining community had become respectable. He looked down across the sweep of gently rolling land, where corrals filled with cattle, others with horses stretched beyond the main street.

He left Zabuca stabled, and then directed the driver to the Dawson Hotel, which boasted a sink in each of its rooms. The two-story building catered to railroad workers, and wandering cowboys. The man at the front desk eyed him as inconspicuously as possible. Mort did not fit the bill of either of those types.

The tall stranger wore plain clothing, well made, but not ostentatious. Clear blue eyes stared out from a tanned face, and he sported only a mustache, different from the beard and mutton chop styles favored by most men. Thin-lipped and square-jawed, he looked little like the teenage boy who told a dark story around a campfire on Fort Phantom Hill, almost thirty years before.

Loud conversation filled the lobby, and candlelight winked from a chandelier overhead. Mort took the last room. The hotel manager asked him to sign the register. In a conversational tone, he related a recent discovery of silver on the rim of the North Park, not too far from Laramie that prompted an influx into town. Mort nodded, and didn't make any comment. He took the room key and draped his saddlebag over a shoulder. With the other hand picked up a small portmanteau with the rifle scabbard lodged between the handles. The man behind the desk observed him with curious eyes as his form ascended the stairs.

The rain disappeared leaving overcast skies, and once inside the room Mort lighted an oil lamp that stood on a small desk. He glanced out the window to the road below, where humanity made their way, each to their own destiny.

The night, always patient waited outside the batwing doors of the Red Light Saloon. In a dark corner, Mort sat at a small table with his back to the wall. A low window next to where he sat allowed him a clear view of the street outside.

A piano player in the opposite corner plonked out a ribald song, and dance hall girls flirted with miners, gamblers and cowboys alike. The men paid for a dance, and then the girls would steer them to the bar to partake of a water-downed drink. The funk of unwashed bodies, and cheap perfume mingled in the rising heat from kerosene lamps. Behind the mahogany bar hung a large mirror that reflected bearded men gathered as they raised a toast here and there. Spittoons lined a foot-rail by their boots.

A card game dominated the attention of many, thanks to the cussing and belligerent attitude of one player who everyone knew as Monte Jim, a card shark and desperado out of Abilene, Kansas.

Mort's face remained impassive when he looked at the group slapping down cards, but one gift he received from being a living pocket included the ability to see harbingers of death when they swirled around a living thing. One crawled up on Monte Jim's lap.

He bellowed over to the bartender, "Send me over a bottle of coffin varnish, I feel Lady Luck is smiling on me tonight. "

A greedy smile that didn't quite reach his eyes exposed yellowed teeth as he pulled the winnings in the middle of the table towards him.

One player attempted to get up and leave. "Where you goin' you chucklehead?" growled Monte Jim. "Off to sit in the corner and bat your eyes at what's going on here?"

"Naw Jim, I just don't have no ballast to keep playing." The miner scraped his chair back from the table and left.

Whatever sat on Jim's lap now draped tentacles around his shoulders in a caressing manner. Mort doubted the man who left understood why he acted on the need to distance himself from the vicinity of the card game; lack of money did not figure into it.

Mort poured himself another shot of whiskey from a bottle that sat in the middle of the table. One reason alone brought him to Laramie; a prostitute named Ruby Summerfield, better known as Ruby Red Lace. He saved her life when she worked for one of the most high-end brothels in San Francisco's Barbary Coast.

Katie Sotharn the madam of the establishment known as Kate's catered to a clientele with deep pockets. However, money alone could not guarantee entry. Lonely sailors and grifters were not welcomed. Discerning men who wanted to smoke a good cigar, and have the loveliest girls entertain them were given admittance. New clients were only allowed with references in hand. This exclusivity usually protected her girls from being too roughed up, or even killed. Kate prided herself on providing the most beautiful girls available in San Francisco's demimonde.

At Kate's, Mort cornered something that only the week before killed a housewife soon after her husband and son left their home. The family lived in a house about one hundred feet from the edge of the Masonic cemetery, and under the shadow of the cross on Lone Mountain. A neighbor found the woman's body in a large circle of blood and slush, her long skirts hiked over her knees. Blood streaked the table, chairs and walls; nearby they found a hatchet covered with hair and gore. Her wounds showed that the perpetrator keep using it on her head long after he killed her. The newspapers never publicized it, but the killer engaged in sex with the body after she died.

The devilish effects of the killer's touch surfaced soon after the murder. Police surgeon Stivers who completed the autopsy on the woman's body, found his left hand swelled soon after. He fell ill, and when the city physician Dr. Blach attended him, he could not identify what poisoned the surgeon's blood. Dr. Stivers took six months to recover, and return to his duties.

Tipped off about the gruesome murder, Mort waited under the shadowiness of trees that lined the perimeter of the Odd Fellows Cemetery, and the adjoining Masonic Cemetery. The poorly populated area, more desolate than usual after the crime lay still under the blanket of night. Not long after moonrise, he saw a figure that skulked down the hill. It walked as a man, then would hunch down, raise its face to the moon and growl in a fashion unlike any human.

Mort distinguished a voice inside of his mind that said one word, "Kyoki". He understood then what he pursued.

Kyoki soldier demons were brutal, and sadistic. They became a rare sight after the Inquisition of the 15th and 16th century. Vultures of grief and suffering, they favored vessels that were criminals or mentally unstable, driving these humans towards further acts of lawlessness or madness. Those who turned their emotions inwards or suffered in silence fed or called the Kyoki even more.

The figure sniffed the air, straightened up and adjusted its clothing. Further down the hill, the lights of houses danced like fireflies in the night. It walked towards them as Mort trailed behind, making sure to stay hidden in pockets of dimness.

Ema filled his mind with scenes that played out like recovered memories that unfolded behind his eyes, tutoring him about the nature of the demon he pursued. It sought prey, and fought being contained inside a human shell since it usually stalked battlefields. It had no need to disguise itself. Those who recovered from their wounds, and described seeing something from hell walking among the dead, were thought to be suffering from delirium brought on by their injuries. However, when there were no battles, the Kyoki joined with those who would spill blood on its behalf.

Mort suspected that it arrived in San Francisco from one of the many ships that docked from different ports of call. Now that he confirmed this human being acted under the control of a demon, Mort aimed to follow it to ground and allow Ema to confront it. This demon didn't stay long with their pocket before discarding it, leaving the human shell a raving lunatic which many times destroyed itself. Ema stirred within him, as if preparing for battle. If this were only a man, then Mort would have dispatched him in a variety of ways.

The figure approached a large mansion sitting amongst a wealth of trees, where music filtered from within. Candlelight flickered from all the windows. A discreet red lantern hung outside the entrance identified it as a brothel, but not a common whorehouse judging by the horseflesh attended to by a stable boy. No doubt, only wealthy men were seeking entertainment within its walls.

The figure walked around the perimeter of the grounds, and stood in the gloom outside the kitchen towards the back of the property. Deep sills holding pots of geraniums and daisies decorated wide windows. A door stood open allowing heat from the cooking fires to escape; beyond it, a pool of light fell upon three steps that led to a small courtyard and gardens. Mort saw servants moving inside the room.

He inched closer in the darkness trying to anticipate what the man planned to do. The figure looked upwards, and he saw what caught its attention. On a small balcony that overlooked the garden, a young woman with a scarlet, low cut dress stood staring out into the night. She touched fingers to her bruised lips, and then turned around to look back into her room. The dark figure scuttled across the grounds, and then in one fluid movement climbed the wall of the house with fingers that were abnormally long. It pulled itself up the wall in a slithering motion that made the body appear to be boneless.

Mort realized he had no time to lose. He ran from the darkness in through the open door of the kitchen, pushing a fat, elderly woman out of the way. A gap-toothed maidservant screamed and ran out the door into the garden beyond.

Mort bound up the narrow servants' stairs in the back of the house. He burst into the hallway of the second floor, and immediately heard the screaming. A woman dressed only in a black corset peered from the entrance of a room across the passage. He overheard a man's voice tell her to come back inside, and shut the door. Mort saw another woman dressed in an emerald gown at the foot of the stairs, looking up at him in surprise. He came to the door of the room he guessed belonged to the girl on the balcony, and threw it open. His unannounced entrance saved her life.

The girl stumbled back onto the bed, and the man crouched above her holding a straight razor in one hand. He swung it down in an arc, but she pushed against him as Mort strode in and the razor cut into her neck, but not deep enough to kill her.

The man stood and faced Mort. His features were dark and strong-boned, and he wore the traditional garb of a sailor. The whites of his eyes were completely red, and he hissed gutturally at Mort. His black hair waved around his head as if he stood inside an invisible sea.

Mort glanced to the woman who held her neck with both hands. Blood trickled from between her fingers. He heard heavy footsteps running up the stairs, and voices calling, "Ruby, Ruby!"

The killer looked at the door, and it slammed shut by itself. Mort heard the lock turn, and then the people outside it were pounding on the wood calling the woman's name.

These events happened in seconds, and then time slowed to a crawl. Inside his body, Ema pushed him back and she instead of him, looked out through his eyeballs.

The man still holding the razor bared his teeth, and crouched down licking its blood-splattered fingers. He stopped all movement, and sniffed the air, swiveling his eyes around until they fixed steadily and unblinkingly on Mort's face. It whimpered like an animal that suffered severe beatings and feared another thrashing.

Ema returned control of Mort's body to him. If she confronted the demon now, it would leave him incapacitated, and unable to help the woman who looked at him with beseeching eyes. She needed medical attention right away. An antidote also had to be administered, otherwise in a few days she would die from a strange fever or blood poisoning.

The Kyoki demon's pocket sensed the change, and with a growl dove out the balcony and into the grounds below. The unnatural silence that encapsulated the tableau fled, and a wave of noise flooded in. The sound of shoulders being put to the door thundered in the room, and then unexpectedly it unlocked, sending two men sprawling onto the floor.

Mort stepped over them, and in one movement tore strips from the bedcover. He pressed them into the woman's neck to staunch the flow of blood. The would-be rescuers were bewildered as the room filled with other people who believed that Mort attacked Ruby. She shook her head, and in a voice above a whisper assured them he had not.

In a short amount of time, the house quieted down as the clientele left the brothel, not wanting to be present when the police arrived. Inconspicuously Mort administered a small amount of salve that he carried in a vial, to a fresh bandage that he placed around Ruby's neck. Only certain apothecary shops, specializing in strange plants and herbs supplied the ingredients.

He told the madam he became aware of Ruby screaming and came to assist, but he thought it wiser if he left before the police arrived. She nodded, understanding too well his insistence on maintaining his anonymity. Before he left the room, he whispered to Ruby that he would visit her in a few days. Their eyes met in understanding.

A week later Mort made plans to check on Ruby. Sun streaked down into a courtyard dominated by a fountain that splashed cool water from a boy riding a dolphin. A stable boy stood outside the two-story, adobe house and held out Zabuca's reins to Mort. He mounted and rode off, soon finding himself among carriages, and the tides of humanity that walked the streets of San Francisco.

A far off bell tower struck noon when he arrived at the brothel. The gap-toothed maid showed Mort into a small parlor. She looked at him with eyes as big as saucers. As he expected, there were no clients about, and most of the girls were still asleep or lounging in their rooms. Red damask curtains, hardwood furniture and the finest carpets created an ambience of refinement. Expensive French wallpaper lined the walls, and a hand-painted screen of a semi-nude woman graced the mantel over the fireplace

A few minutes later, the maid led him to Ruby's room. He cut a dashing figure, freshly shaved and wearing a buckskin jacket. The prostitute eyed him appreciatively as she rested with her neck swathed in bandages. Her blonde hair teetered on her head, held only by a thin, yellow ribbon. She lounged on the bed wearing an embroidered morning gown.

He saw the curiosity glinting in her eyes. She wanted to know about her attacker, but he also sensed she looked at him trying to determine another reason for his visit.

She looked up at him through her eyelashes; her voice still raspy and asked, "Would you like to see me again?"

"I am glad to see you are better, I know that this could have been much worse." Mort pointedly did not answer her question.

"Yes, I know, but things have changed for me. That man didn't kill me, but... he's damaged me." she said with a resigned sigh.

Mort raised inquiring brows.

"Kate likes her girls to wear pretty gowns that show off your goods so the gentlemen boast about how beautiful we are, and bring in more men to come and spend some time with us." she simpered with a slight smile on her lips.

"But now, it's all changed for me." Her smile faded as she pulled down the bandage, and showed him a livid red cut that marred her white neck. Another one ran across her chest. No doubt, it would scar her when the injuries healed. Ruby could no longer be considered a top shelf whore.

Beautiful could not be used to describe her. Ruby's facial features were too strong, and only her youth softened her nose and wide mouth, and made her somewhat pretty. In five or six years, this effect would fade. Her one indisputable attraction lay in her pearly skin, luminescent and without blemish, until now.

Mort considered that these circumstances were favorable towards the real reason he visited Ruby. He knew that once a human survived an attack by one of these creatures, an invisible mark on them would draw others to her. He deliberated how to convince her to leave San Francisco within a short amount of time.

"Ruby, I will leave San Francisco to travel to the East on business, but I worry about your wellbeing. They have not caught the attacker." the tall man said matter-of-factly.

Mort saw her shudder and her face paled, "I've thought of that," she replied.

"I know someone out in the Wyoming Territory. Her name is Gussie Telfair; she runs a house out of Laramie. She treats her girls well, and I will send word ahead of your arrival. She will give you work, no questions asked. Your injuries will not matter to her."

Ruby looked at Mort's face, and realized that any hope of becoming his mistress did not exist. He extended only kindness to her, something she received little of in her life, and she recognized the sentiment. She understood he did not expect sexual favors in return.

Ruby bit her lip and considered what he proposed, knowing that she her options were limited. The cheap bordellos above the countless saloons by the wharf were not to her liking. These places did not welcome gentlemen who came to be plied with champagne and a coquettish phrase before going upstairs. Mort followed the different emotions warring upon her face.

The drone of cicadas filled the silence of the afternoon as sunlight slanted in through the open balcony doors.

"Ruby, do not ask me how I know this, but I feel that it is not safe for you to stay in San Francisco," he said in a soft drawl.

Their eyes locked, and Ruby understood without asking further that he understated the danger of her situation. Despite convincing herself in the days since her attack that her imagination had run away with her, she feared that something unholy tried to murder her.

"I'll go." she simply stated.

Mort stood up and placed a fifty-dollar gold note on the table next to her.

"I will make plans to get you there, and have someone escort you safely to Gussie's establishment. You will receive the details later today."

She grabbed his hand, and brought it to her cheek and then kissed the top of it. "Thank you," she whispered.

Mort left the parlor house, and rode towards Gray's Undertakers, located on Divisadero Street. He had eyes and ears there who alerted him to corpses that exhibited a strange death.

San Francisco thrived and grew by the day, and in 1879, it boasted almost a quarter million inhabitants. The busy street bustled with carriages; men wearing top hats and women carrying parasols went about their business. Mort saw a swell of humanity where an inhuman spirit could find a weak or willing vessel with ease.

Mort stopped at a corner to adjust his hat when a teenage boy waved his hand, calling his attention. The messenger shaded his eyes as he looked up at Mort who reached down from the saddle to take a folded piece of paper from him. He passed a coin to the boy who dashed off into the crowd with payment in hand. The teenager delivered messages from the undertaker, but he also brought Mort tidbits of information that he espied on the streets. He knew that Mr. Peccatum paid generously when provided with darker stories, which most of the newspapers in the city would refuse to print.

The message read:

An Englishman named Benjamin Hallett about 30 years of age, one of the crew of the ship Black Hawk committed suicide last night by stabbing himself to the heart in Franklin's sailor boarding house on Clark Street. He arrived here from China about 2 weeks ago and during his stay, many complained of hearing him hold a conversation in a room where he was the only occupant. He smells as if he rolled around in a slaughterhouse and if he had not done away with himself, he would soon have died from starvation. I do not believe he has eaten since he left his ship. PK

The undertaker's assistant, Paul Kane sent him this note, because he found the condition of the body and the circumstances of the death unusual.

Mort knew before long, the Kyoki demon would demand his pocket spill his own blood as a farewell gift. In a port city, infamous for its tenderloin area known as the Barbary Coast, this demon could be anywhere, and he suspected it would leave in any direction that would take it out of Ema's reach.

III. Prudence's Redemption

WEEKS PASSED AND THE CITY of San Francisco persevered in its normal cycle of life, death and the infamy of its demimonde. Mort continued to hunt with and for Ema, immersed in the murky world of occultism that flowed like a hidden stream below the depravities found in places where humans congregate. Ruby became a distant memory, until one day when he received a letter from Laramie.

May 29th, 1879
Laramie, Wyoming Territory

Dear Mort,

I have intended writing to you for some days past, but did not do so because I heard that the mail was not getting to San Francisco because of late snowfall and some changes they had made in the stage route, however my news is too important and I could not delay writing any longer.

I will say this with as few words as possible. Ruby Summerfield arrived here safely, and I found a place for her as you asked. We all felt sorry for the girl. She acted sick or rather feeble, but we soon realized she feigned herself very much worse than she actually was in order to excite sympathy.

My first thought was that I needed to take her in hand, and let her understand that she must stay where she is placed, unless something of this kind is done I could no longer be called upon to take care of her, not because she has nothing to support herself with, but because men are not willing to be pestered with her ever, much less pay to spend time with her.

I do not believe she understands that if she lived by herself, she would not be able to buy food or wood, but would stay cold and without anything to eat which I do not believe she could stand it for long.

Since the first days when she arrived here, her character has changed. If anyone inquires about how she gets along, she will insult them and say she can take care of herself and don't thank anybody for looking after her. She knows everything; she can't be advised, she is wiser than seven men that can render a reason.

Despite my warnings, she just gave it a lick and a promise and I am afeared that who she keeps company with will come to no good end.

It all started when one who calls himself John Schwartze came looking for a girl. You know I've kept a bed-house for many a year, and I knew from the moment I clapped eyes on this feller he was trouble. There's just something off about him. Even the threat of a lacing didn't make no difference, and I noticed he wouldn't take his eyes off Ruby. He finally left.

The celestial that brings me firewood saw him, and told me something that made my blood run cold. He said that his real name is Packer. That's the man that back in the winter of '74 ate five men traveling with him. He escaped from Saguache after they sentenced him. Coming from me, you understand that I don't want to stir things up and have the law here.

Ruby had a conniption fit when I told her I won't have him here. She was mad enough to spit in the devil's eye; she went off to work at the Three Mile hog ranch outside Fort Laramie, and then she left there and went to the Red Light Saloon.

I've heard she's been keeping company with Packer. I write this plainly to you in order that you may know what the situation is.

I have told you all I know and perhaps more beside so I will close by telling you I'm afeared the next time I see Ruby she'll be in a cold meat wagon on the way to the bone orchard. I've never forgotten what you did for me and mine. I am still your friend, Gussie Telfair.

In response to the letter, Mort found himself at the Red Light Saloon watching the stairs through a smoke-filled haze. He did not have long to wait before Ruby stood on the landing surveying the room below. She laughed and whispered to another girl standing next to her. The blue dress she wore set off the red ribbon around her neck. A plunging neckline exposed her full breasts, and a hem that came down to mid-shin with a black ruffled petticoat underneath, tossed when she danced. Ruby made no effort to disguise the red scars that made a roadmap on her neck and chest.

Descending the stairs, she saw Mort and her smile faded. She made her way through the crowd, brushing away several men that tried to grab her by the waist and dance with her.

"So, you here for a frolic?" She said in a flirtatious tone that didn't quite reach her eyes.

"No Ruby, I'm here to see you." Mort pulled a chair out for her. Now that she sat close to him, he confirmed how much she had transformed in the few months since their last meeting. Changes not for the better; her eyes were wild and defiant, and her youthful prettiness had disappeared. An impatient twist to her lips, spelled only trouble.

Mort lied to her about why he came to Laramie. He suspected she would not appreciate being bait.

"Man has to get out, time to time," He replied with his steel blue eyes twinkling.

"I suppose."

"Didn't like working for Gussie?" Mort asked her as he tossed off another drink.

Ruby twirled a curl around her finger, looking down at the table. In an evasive tone she responded, "She's too bossy, and didn't let a girl have fun."

Mort stood up. Ruby looked up at his six foot, two inch frame, and despite her experience the night they met; she now felt the quiet danger that exuded from him.

"Let's go up to a room, that way we can catch up on old times," he said with a faint smile.

Ruby looked at him with a curious glint in her eye, "Is that a bluff, or do you mean it for real play?"

Mort became brusque, and with cynical amusement said, "Ruby for being a mab, you ask a lot of questions."

Ruby shot up from the chair and stared at something over Mort's shoulder. He turned around and saw who he assumed to be the madam. She glared at Ruby, her lips set in a thin line of displeasure.

Ruby tossed her head and took him by the hand pulling him along towards the stairs, all for the benefit of the older woman watching them. The woman's gaze then swept downwards among the girls dancing and circulating among the men, making sure that all of them were loosening their pockets.

She put out her hand when Mort stood next to her on the landing. "It'll be a dollar, mister."

He handed over the coin, and as Ruby passed by her, the woman grabbed her roughly by the arm. She whispered loudly, "Girl, if I see you dawdlin' again waiting for that queer fish to show up, you'll find yourself pirooting back at Three Mile. You understand me?" The woman shoved her towards Mort.

Ruby led Mort to one of the rooms that lined the hallway. An iron four-poster bed crouched in the corner; next to it stood a changing screen and a chair. At the opposite corner, a spindly table with a washbasin, and a small fly-specked mirror hanging above it, crowded into the chamber.

Ruby leaned into Mort, pushing her breasts up against his chest. "I thought you'd forgotten all about me. I figured you were out drinkin' champagne from some lady's slipper in New York somewhere."

She smiled up at him and looped her arms around his neck. The sexual tension broke when from the other side of the door they made out a man's hoarse whisper, "Ruby! Ruby girl, you in there?"

"Expecting company?" Mort looked down at Ruby. Panic erased the flirtatious smile on her face. She shushed him as she brought a trembling finger to her lips.

Mort raised his voice, "Partner you'll have to come back another day, I think I'll keep this twofer with me all night long."

"Ruby, open up, who's in there with you?" The same coarse voice took on a menacing tone. The doorknob jiggled violently.

Mort pushed Ruby away, yanked open the door and in a grim, tight voice said, "Are you deaf you son of a bitch?"

There stood a bearded, scruffy man dressed like a miner, that stank as if it had been years since his last bath. He looked much older than his thirty-some years of age. The man's eyes bugged out of his head, and then his face darkened. Mort grabbed him by the shirtfront and the man balled his hand into a fist. Then he stopped the motion of his arm, and hissed at Mort like a cat.

The madam with a fierce frown trudged down the hallway, looking madder than an old, wet hen. She intended to make things right. When she looked up and saw both men, she opened her mouth to start a tongue-lashing, and then she took wise counsel from her birth name, which happened to be Prudence. She stopped in her tracks, and closed her mouth with a snap. Her eyes squinted because in the dim light of the passage she thought she saw a green halo around the tall stranger's fair head.

Mort looked her straight in the eye. "You need to make tracks right back to that landing, and let me solve this problem for you. He is a problem isn't he?"

"He surely is. Eager for a poke, but no tin to pay for it." the madam complained.

"Well, before I ask for my dollar back Prudence, you pretend it's business as usual, and all you're doing is making sure your whore is earning her keep." She understood without being told that he would brook no argument.

Prudence nodded her head, thinking she would need some extra drops of laudanum later that night. She wondered how this stranger got hold of her Christian name. Prudence couldn't help but furtively cross herself in an imitation of her Irish mammie.

Mort pulled the miner into the room, slammed the door closed and threw him into the chair. Ruby leaped to stand between the men, piercing Mort with a look that could have put him six feet under if it were a weapon.

"Mort what are you doing? I'm not your property; I can be with whoever I want to be. How much do you think that dollar bought you?" Her voice full of fury and spit screeched.

The whore's face transformed, and her scars throbbed a maroon red. Mort moved her aside with an arm, keeping his eyes on the man who called himself John Schwartze.

He taunted the miner, "You always let a woman do your fighting for you?"

The man stood up, and with a hard shove sent Ruby crashing into the opposite side of the room. Then Mort saw what he waited for. The man's face transformed. The nose flattened, and the pupil in each eye lengthened. The iris grew and blotted out any white left in the eyeball. An inhuman, rumbling growl grew in the man's chest.

Ruby launched herself again between the two men. "Leave him be!" she screamed at Mort, attempting to claw at his eyes.

Mort looked at her face, and saw madness. She slid to the floor and grabbed Schwartze's pant leg letting out a hysterical cry. Ruby looked up at Mort, and saw the look of a hunter setting his sight on a prey. She shook her head, and ran behind the screen in the corner.

The dancing shadows cast by the oil lamp took on weird and humanoid shapes. Mort saw a man in the grip of a dark spirit, and in response, Ema pulsed inside of him.

"So Packer, that is your real name right? Decided yet, which are the best cuts of meat on Ruby are? Hard to explain that away, not like the five men you killed in Colorado. You'll be the guest of honor at a necktie party for sure... Packer." Mort emphasized his name, and then hit him.

Packer staggered backwards, and Mort stepped in and whipped a wicked left into his jaw. Mort's savagery caught him unaware since until then he only talked. He backed away, but Mort gave him no chance to recover. Another left to the belly this time, and then a right. Packer flailed at him, but Mort stepped outside of his reach and then drove a fist aimed at his kidney area. Packer grunted with a growling undertone, and then plunged after Mort trying to topple him off his feet. Mort stepped backwards and then forward into a punch that caught Packer on the chin, and then a second punch to his mouth. Blood spilled over Packer's greasy shirt from the cut on his lip.

Packer stood there, looking at Mort up and down, realizing the tall man breathed regularly and intended to keep beating him. Mort looked at Ruby who stood with her hands to her side; her eyes brimmed with fury.

Mort noticed Packer blinked furiously. His face returned to its normal human appearance, and then he dropped to the floor without an attempt to break his fall. All his limbs convulsed, and he arched his back in the throes of a seizure.

Ruby screamed a high-pitched sound of despair, and when Mort turned to her, she held a small derringer that she hid in the folds of her skirt. She aimed it at Mort, pulled the trigger and shot him in the head.

A dull thump followed the crack of the shot, as the pistol slipped from Ruby's grip and dropped to the rough planks. She ignored Packer who writhed on the floor, and instead her brain tried to make sense of what she saw unfold before her eyes. An infinite, echoing silence filled the small room. A naked woman with bluish skin, which glistened with pearls of moisture, caught Mort's body before it hit the floor. Blood sprinkled down to a pool that widened on the wooden planks beneath it.

The woman's hair long and wet, shone with a rich burgundy color. It made a curtain that covered her face as she bent down, and laid Mort's head with the utmost gentleness on the floor. She placed her hand over a bleeding wound on the side of his skull. The blood ceased to trickle out. Ema made a circular motion with her hand and then whispered words that Ruby did not understand. A golden light encircled Mort, as it lengthened it took on a transparent texture of feathers that covered his entire body, which ended in a misty eagle's head over his face.

When the woman straightened, she held a whip in her hand that she cracked, and in the blink of an eye, it transformed the quarters over the saloon. It became a low-ceilinged room with beams of dark wood overhead. The woman's skin turned a normal pink color. Her hair now dry, fluffed out around her body.

Ruby's legs gave out under her, and she tried to scramble into the corner, but instead bumped into Packer who lay drooling from his mouth.

The faint aroma of ionization filled the space. A huge, well-polished bronze mirror materialized from the edges of the chamber, filling the space from ceiling to floor. The woman swept her hand down in front of her and a white, shimmering cloth encircled her body, leaving her full, pink-tipped breasts partially exposed on either side.

Dizziness engulfed Ruby when the woman turned her piercing green eyes on her. Then something leathery grabbed her arm, and she wished at that moment that she could will herself to faint. A creature three feet tall, with greenish skin and jagged teeth leaned up next to her. It rubbed its face against hers. Then a long black tongue, sticky with saliva came out of its mouth, and swept across the scar on her neck and chest.

The crack of the whip made the air sizzle, and the creature jumped back, crouching in abject terror.

Ema said, "Imp, I said protect."

A low whimper made Ruby look next to her, and she saw Packer, now conscious stare in horror at a similar creature that sidled close to him.

Ema stepped up to the bronze mirror, and with the tip of the whip hit it; a deep, humming sound filled the room. A low mewling filled the silence that followed. It sounded like a newborn kitten, and then turned into the scream of an animal in heat. Gleaming eyes flashed from the darkness under the bed. Ema hit the bronze mirror once again, and the deep bong heightened to the purest bell-like tone.

The creature cried out in pain, and then crawled out into the middle of the room. It unfolded its body until it stood on two, hind legs, its feline head brushed up against the ceiling. A leathery tail whipped behind it, and two pendulous breasts covered in fur hung from its chest. A thin mixture of brown fur and human-like hair covered the rest of its body.

Ema cracked the whip, and the creature dropped to all four and hissed at her. The fur on its back rose, and it looked up at the woman with pure hatred.

It conversed in a language understood by none, and all at the same time. "Mercy, oh Sibyl, I have surrendered its flesh."

"You surrendered it because that man's brain is diseased. I cannot grant you what I do not have to give. I can only understand that you are true to your nature, as I am to mine."

The creature sat on its haunches, and with its hind leg scratched itself behind the ear. A woman's genitals covered in hair flashed between its legs.

It turned back to the woman, unable to look at her face, and then continued, "I have stayed away from the place of men. This man called out to me. It cried out that it would make any agreement so it could fill its belly, but I know what it hungered for, and it was not sustenance for its body. Of all those men there, I knew it was of my kind."

The woman cracked the whip, and the imps ran behind the humans they were protecting. Each looked over the shoulder of Ruby and Packer, their eyes following the line of blue light that lingered in the air where the lash arced through space. The scent of lilac filled the room.

Ema looked down at the elemental that now crouched on all fours, its tufted ears flattened to its head. It made a slobbering sound as its thick tongue licked its muzzle, baring pointed teeth and long fangs.

"The dead have come to me, and asked for your return. The Old Ones gave you what you asked for, the scent of death upon the wind, the sorrow of the ones who loved them; they understood the living had no place there. In exchange, you would guard their resting place and make sure their bones would be undisturbed." Ema's voice held a note of finality.

"Very well," it hissed, and then slyly looked over its shoulder at Ruby, "but let me have the woman. I will trouble you no more, I will return to my place in the cold earth, and fulfill my pledge to the Old Ones."

"Do you seek to bargain with me?" Ema asked, her voice sounded no longer human, but echoed and vibrated with a bell-like quality.

The elemental raised itself on its two hind legs; it pointed ears brushed the ceiling. It swung its head back and forth, and mewled in pain. The shadows on the walls leapt with a life of their own, and the two imps tittered. One of them gave Ruby's upper arm a vicious pinch, and then whispered in her ear, "What a sweet morsel you will be."

"Cease, Walker between the Worlds," the elemental cried out. "I will bury her bones deep in my lair, and keep them safe. Her shade will converse with me. Grant me this one parting gift, and our paths will never cross again." Saliva slavered from its lower lip.

"No." Ema said.

It growled down at the woman, angry but unable to defy her.

The whip in Ema's hand stiffened and became a staff, she tapped it hard on the ground and it turned a deep, verdant green. Shoots sprouted from it, then leaves and buds, and in seconds flowers bloomed, their lush and heady scent filling the space. In the center of some flowers, there were tiny faces, some blinked, others smiled. Tendrils of leafy vines extended from the staff and then wound themselves gently around Ema's hair.

The elemental crouched down on all fours, covering its face with its large paws. It mewled again like a small kitten. Its leathery tail curled around its hindquarters. Ema stepped forward and towered over it.

"The woman can never be yours. She is a life-giver. Through her body, spirits incarnate in human form; no doubt you would use her as an instrument of death luring the unwary to damnation."

The imps cowered behind the humans, listening to the exchange. The imp next to Packer whispered in his ear, "Doesn't it smell like excrement in here?"

Packer looked at the thing, then at Ruby who grabbed his hand, squeezing it hard. She sat close to him, her lips so pale they faded into the whiteness of her drawn face. The imp sidled up next to Ruby, stuck its tongue out at Packer and cackled.

Ema said tersely, "Leaena you have forgotten you are Destruction, she is Creation. In exchange for your avarice, I will return you to where you belong, and those who you abandoned will have dominion over you until you are never tempted to forswear yourself again."

Ema struck the staff on the ground, and in the twinkling of an eye, it lost its rigidity and became a whip once again. The flowers and leaves disintegrated, and the ones in her hair formed themselves into a crown around her head.

The elemental shrank, curled around itself.

Ema looked at Ruby and Packer, and told them in a quiet voice, "Close your eyes."

To the imps, "Make sure they do not see."

The scaly creatures crouched behind each human, and put their hands over their eyes. The one behind Ruby nuzzled the nape of her neck, and inhaled deeply. It whispered, "What a waste."

With her left hand, Ema drew a circle of light in the air, and then within it she drew a sigil that glowed. She said only one word, "Alu". Skeletal arms extended from the circle of light and the bony hands grabbed the elemental, and drew it back into the circle and then into the darkness beyond.

The circle closed in upon itself, evaporating as the edges of the room grew misty, and shimmered in multicolored stars.

Ema's clothing, the mirror and whip were sucked into a small circle where no light penetrated. She extended her arm, palm up and the dark circle jump into the center of her hand like a living thing. It vanished with a pop that made the glass in the window tremble in its frame. The mirror over the basin, cracked, and the shards fell into it.

Ema stood naked in the middle of the room. She kneeled next to Mort, and passed her hand over his body. The golden envelope evaporated, and like a child, she lifted him and placed him on the bed. She touched the blood that soaked his shirtfront, and the lapel of his coat. Ema bowed her head, and closed her eyes, thinking if she delayed less than a moment the metal projectile would have embedded itself into his brain. A deep, heart-wrenching despair pierced her to the core at the thought of losing Mort. The agony perplexed her, but she could not deny it engulfed her being.

Behind her, she heard the imps bickering, "You ask her".

"No, you ask her."

"Didn't you see what happened the last time someone asked for the woman? She might turn me to stone, and place me in some cathedral or monastery where it would be an eternity of prayers, incense and lots of chanting. No!" It cried out in alarm.

"She doesn't know." the other imp warned.

"What don't I know?" Ema rounded on the imps.

"Sibyllina, the woman is polluted. Life cannot grow in her womb. All we ask is that you allow us to accompany her during her remaining years of life. A little torment never hurt a daughter of Eve," one imp said in a wheedling voice.

Encouraged by Ema's silence they came closer to her. She then shifted her gaze to Ruby who sat next to Packer on the floor. Both of their faces wore dazed expressions.

She stepped over the imps, and they both skittered into the darkness under the bed. Ema grabbed Ruby by the hair, and pulled her up to a standing position. She then dragged the screaming woman, who tried with desperate hands to loosen Ema's grip, towards the washbasin. She pulled out a shard of the mirror, and held it in front of Ruby's rage-filled face.

The younger woman stilled as if enthralled with her own reflection. She stared at her eyes as if hypnotized, and then fell to her knees and coughed. She threw her head back, and her eyes rolled upwards. Out of her mouth emerged a large crow. It jumped out and perched itself on the rim of the basin, pecking at the shiny pieces of glass that lay at the bottom.

A pocket within a pocket; Ema realized that she blamed Ruby's defiance on the effects of the demon that attacked her in San Francisco, and then her attraction to Packer and his dark passenger.

The crow then looked at her, it's beady, black eyes more intelligent than a normal bird would be. It cocked its head, as if reading her mind.

Ema recognized this as a Trezor underling; a spiritual bottom feeder, known for its ability to pocket animals, especially disease-carrying rats or birds. Alchemists in 18th century Hungary described them as bone demons that subsisted off human corpses. Being lesser spirits, they lurked in the darkest or most isolated parts of a city, feeding off the sick and homeless. They were crafty and malevolent, but their petty nature and hatred of their betters limited their ambition. Usually found in the company of Incubi or other greater spirits, they served for reward or through coercion. It made a perfect spy.

Ema strode over to the window and opened it. The bird flew out into the night. She realized this served as a lesson in humility, when two lowly imps recognized what she failed to see, a human being manipulated by a dark spirit. Something wanted to separate her from one of the most powerful avatars to hunt with her. It sought to make her the prey, not the pursuer. In an existence fraught with constant danger, she recognized that something truly menacing lurked around her.

Ruby sat back on her heels, and cried in silence. Ema looked down at her and thought, "That's a good sign."

Luckily, she used imps to guard these tainted humans, Ema thought, otherwise Ruby would have attempted to finish Mort off. She clapped her hands, and the constant, inarticulate chatter from the imps, dropped off into an echoing silence.

Ema pulled Ruby up by her elbow, and Packer scrambled to his feet at the same time. She pointed at Packer, and told him a low voice, "You will leave this place, and never come looking for Ruby again. No one will believe you if you speak of what you saw. You will spend your days either in prison, or an asylum."

"No, ma'am," he mumbled, trying to look at her face, but his eyes would drift down to her nudity, and then back up. Her body curved along regal lines.

Ema turned to Ruby, who stopped crying and looked on with reddened yes. "Do you have a cloak?"

"Yes I do, but I put it away with my nicer gowns. Those were happy days when I lived in San Francisco." Ruby's eyes welled again with tears. Packer reached out, and tried to touch her hand. She pulled away, and shot him a withering glance. He in turn gave her a brutal, and unfriendly stare.

Ruby turned away to open a small steamer trunk hidden behind the table, and Ema unbolted the door for Packer. The hallway lay in darkness. He clomped down the passage mumbling in a loud voice. He brushed by Prudence, and she gaped at him with startled eyes. When she looked up the hallway, she saw the white body of what looked like a nude woman who stepped back into the room. Neither Ruby nor any of her other girls looked like her.

All night long, she felt a cold breeze that swept through the passage. A blue light shimmered out from underneath the door of Ruby's room, and a forbidding pulse had kept her away all night long. Prudence felt unsure what she feared more, the shadowy darkness of the hallway or asking the tall stranger for more coin if he planned to spend the night with Ruby.

A whoop of laughter, smoke and the plinking music of the piano drifted up the stairs. Prudence squared her shoulders, and walked down the passage until she stood before the door. Her skin rose in goose bumps, and she saw her breath steam in front of her face. She raised her hand to knock on the door, and then something moved in the furthest corner of the hallway. She fixed her attention on the spot. Fear, stark and vivid, glittered in her eyes. Out of the cobalt darkness stepped a figure well over seven feet tall that held a spear. Prudence's eyes traveled up to look at its face, and that's when she let out a screech. In place of a human head, something that looked like a dog or a coyote, with pointed ears and an elongated snout stared back at her. She turned and ran as fast as her short, chubby legs would carry her.

Prudence rolled down the stairs, half sliding, half walking all the while reciting the Our Father as loud as her lungs would allow. The bartender Walter threw his towel down in irritation because he suspected Prudence of using too much laudanum.

Several people helped Prudence up when she reached the bottom of the stairs. Panting, her eyes wild, she belted out, "I repent, Jesus, I repent! Take pity on this poor sinner, just save me from the devil! Save me Jesus!"

She shook her finger at the crowd surrounding her, "Leave this den of iniquity before the devil takes your soul, you whoremongers, sons of bitches."

Several men laughed aloud and returned to their drinking and gambling, and the girls looked at each other with knowing glances. Prudence once again recited the Our Father and sped out of the batwing doors into the darkness beyond.

IV. No Country for Cowards

EMA DRAPED HERSELF IN A GRAY WOOL, riding cape with a tasseled hood. Taller than Ruby, it came up only to mid-shin, but it would serve the purpose of hiding her nakedness.

"Ruby is there a way to leave this building that's not through the saloon?" Ema's voice sounded velvet-edged and strong.

"Yes, there's a door off this same floor that leads to stairs in the back, and into the alley. They call it Tiger Alley."

"Gather a few things, and I want you to go to Gussie's house."

"I don't think she'll let me in," Ruby said in a meek voice.

"You say the word "debitio" to her, and tell her that Mort needs her help. She'll stop asking questions after that. Direct her to the alley, and wait with a wagon or anything that I can use to transport Mort. Do you understand?" Ema asked with cool authority.

Ruby nodded. "What about my things?"

"Leave them, they reek of you."

Ruby swallowed, she understood Ema didn't refer to a physical odor, but something much more personal. She grabbed a shawl, and pulled it around her shoulder.

"Ruby, dawn is not far off."

"I understand, and I wanted to thank you for saving my bacon, and… what's your name?"

"Ema."

They stepped into the dim hallway. Ema placed her palm on the door and whispered a few words.

Ruby observed her, and then said in a low voice, "You know the bar dog downstairs likes to come up, and sleep in there sometimes. He might find Mort."

"No, he won't."

Then Ruby saw the same figure Prudence saw earlier that night materialize out of the darkness. She sucked her breath in, and grabbed Ema's hand.

"No he surely won't that poor bastard." Ruby said in a shaky voice.

In the dark alley, Ruby and Ema parted ways. Ema walked through the gloom towards the hotel. Most of the men she encountered were drunk, and could not stand, much less accost a woman.

She found herself behind the hotel where Mort checked in a few hours before. Ema gained access through double doors left ajar for merchants to deliver their merchandise. She walked through the deserted hallway on bare feet, and let herself in using the key she had taken from Mort.

Less than an hour later, Ema looked at her face in the mirror, before she draped a black veil over it. The portmanteau Mort brought stood open, and she retrieved a complete set of widow's weeds. This outfit afforded her a reason to cover her face, and allowed her a modicum of privacy, something essential in a place where men outnumbered women by a considerable amount.

Men tipped their hats to her as she descended the stairs; however, etiquette dictated that they should not approach a lady in mourning. A man who once sailed to ports in Central America recognized the scent of frangipani that drifted in her wake. The black veil that draped over her face and her upper body hid the fact that she did not wear a corset, or any of the underclothes that modesty dictated a woman would never leave her room without donning.

She settled the bill at the front desk, and left instructions for delivery of their belongings to Gussie's address. The man at the desk raised his eyebrows, looked at her over his spectacles and nodded.

When Ema reached the alley behind the Red Light Saloon, a wagon waited there. A young Chinese girl sat holding the reins. Far off several roosters crowed, and the first sounds of humans awakening were borne on the wind.

The girl's face remained impassive as she saw a woman dressed in black, bring down a man cradled like a child in her arms. She stepped down the stairs awkwardly maneuvering his body, and then placed him in the back of the wagon and covered him with a blanket.

Once Ema climbed in and settled next to her, she clucked to the horse and it trotted forward.

Ema looked at her and asked, "What is your name?"

"Jenny."

"Your real name."

The girl glanced at her out of the corner of her eye, and whispered, "Jin Wei".

"Take me to the stables, then take this man back to the house and tell Gussie to make him comfortable. I have things to take care of in the town."

The proprietor at the livery stable, marveled at how the elegantly dressed widow mounted the high-spirited mare like a man. "If ever there was a reason to return from the dead," he thought, "she would be it."

Later that afternoon Ema sat in a darkened room, next to Mort who lay on a bed. He slept soundly with a thick bandage around his head. The bullet grazed the side of his skull deeply, but the threat of losing him had passed. His knuckles split and bruised, lay on the bedclothes.

Ema left the room, and followed Gussie downstairs to a small parlor where she transacted business. Noises were few in the two-story house that sat on the edge of town. Customers did not arrive until nightfall, and most of the girls were asleep. Ema looked at Gussie and saw a raw-boned woman, with fair hair tinged with red and gray. Her cheeks appeared to be perpetually flushed, and she wore a severe gown with a high collar and long sleeves. On a small table close by a meal of bread, meat and coffee waited for them.

Gussie listened as Ema outlined her plans to leave the next day with two mules, a covered wagon and supplies she purchased a few hours before. She looked at Ema, having seen her once over fifteen years before, and the woman looked no different.

Gussie broached a subject that made her tremble with apprehension. "You would not think me a romantic Miss Ema, but I am; and a realist too. Common sense dictates my actions; otherwise, I would end up with many thanks and empty pockets. My sentimental heart has delayed this decision too long."

Her voice shook as she fought to stifle tears, "Take Jenny with you. If you take her with you, you'd be doing me a favor."

A melancholy frown flitted across her features as she continued, "When one of my girls died from too much opium, the celestial who owned her mother gave her to me as the recompense. A scrawny, little thing dressed in rags, he thought he'd pulled a fast one on ol' Gussie. She could hardly walk, and I suspect he thought she'd be dying soon."

Gussie sighed, "As you can see that's not the case anymore. He's asked to buy her back twice, and I've said no, and I'm afeared he'll spirit her away. I've several men ask me when she'll be working with the other girls. The day is fast approaching when I can't protect her anymore."

"What does Jenny want?"

"She wants to live, like any young person wants to, but if she stays here, it won't be much of a life."

Ema stayed quiet, as if pondering her proposition.

"You're taking Ruby to that place in Santa Fe, why can't you take her? Those nuns with running a hospital and an orphanage, surely they need another pair of hands."

"Gussie, has she told you she wants to go?" Ema asked in a low voice.

"We talked about it before, but when she returned with Mort, she came straight to me and said she'll go anywhere with you. I don't know what she saw, but I think Jenny will follow you off the side of a cliff."

"As you wish Gussie, I will write ahead to let them know I am bringing her. I will leave her in the hands of this person, who is a good friend and then her future is in her own hands."

Gussie's face brightened at her words. "Thankee, thankee Miss Ema. What is that person's name so I may write to her and find out about Jenny's wellbeing?"

"Her name is Sister Blandina, and you can find her at St. Vincent's Orphanage."

The next day Ema sat astride Zabuca dressed in trousers, and a buckskin shirt. Her hair hung in a thick braid down her back, and she tied a red scarf around her neck. A wide-brimmed hat shaded her face.

The mules' harnesses jingled as they shook their head waiting to pull the wagon. Jenny sat next to Ruby who held the reins. Ema leaned over once more to look at Mort who rested in a comfortable, makeshift bed inside the wagon.

His eyes were open a slit, and he murmured, "Be careful."

"Always, sleep now," her husky voice, responded first in his mind and then into his ear.

Ema looked at the slumbering man. He breathed deeply, and she suspected he would need all his wits and strength about him in the coming days. She cheated death when she saved him, and that debt would come due sometime in the future. She also hoped to draw out the hidden enemy that instead of running from her instead sent a spy.

Gussie waved her hand in farewell as the wagon pulled out, and a cloud of dust followed it. Next to her stood Mamie, one of the working girls dressed in a corset and thin wrapper. "You sure you want to let Jenny go to Santa Fe? I understood Billy the Kid and other desperados are killing each other out there. There are a lot of wicked people that would eat those three up like they were sweetmeats."

Gussie leaned backwards, crossed her arms and closed her eyes as if offering a silent prayer. "I pity the poor devil who takes it into his head to harm any of them, yes I surely do."

The group traveled through a sapphire and white afternoon, yellow sand stretching off into the horizon. The sun arced downwards through a sky shot through with streaks of violet, when the group stopped, and set up camp. Ema unsaddled Zabuca, and then she heard a high whistling, and saw the shadow of large wings as a golden eagle snatched something from a juniper tree and dropped it at her feet.

A crow, its lifeless eyes stared at Ema as she picked it up. The neck dangled, and a soft breeze ruffled its dark feathers. The foot twitched, and she held out her other hand next to it, palm up. A scaly, snake-like thing slithered there from the crow. It had a dragon's head with two small leathery wings in place of ears.

Ema's eyes narrowed. In answer to a silent dialogue that only she heard, she said, "You'd rather defy me than answer my question. You must fear who sent you a great deal. Ponder in a place of light the error of your choice."

A cube of yellow light spun from one of her fingertips, and then it jumped onto the scaly creature and encased it. It shrunk to the size of a die, and then jumped into Ema's coat pocket.

The golden eagle looked down at Ema from the juniper tree. She threw the body of the crow into the air, and a small burst of fire disintegrated it and the ashes floated off in a breath of wind.

Jenny stood next to Ruby, looking on in silence, her mouth open in disbelief. Ruby pushed her mouth closed with a forefinger, and before she turned away said, "You have seen nothing yet."

"Wouldn't talk, huh?" a gruff voice came from the back of the wagon. Mort sat there, his bare feet dangling down. He squinted across at Ema, an unspoken understanding making words unnecessary.

Ema smiled at him. Mort smiled back. Jin Wei murmured to herself, "This I have seen before. It is love, the complete surrender of the heart."

V. Afterthoughts

ON OCTOBER 17, 1879, the local papers reported that Monte Jim and Henry Brown were playing a game of cards at a saloon in Eagle City, Colorado. They quarreled over a stake of two thousand dollars on the table. They leveled their revolvers and fired three shots apiece. Jim died after being struck by two bullets, one of them in the chest. Gravely injured, Henry fled the town.

In 1883, nine years after he absconded from Saguache, a man acquainted with Alferd Packer recognized him by his laugh. He used the alias John Schwartze. Packer received a second trial. They found him guilty, and he received a death sentence. Because of a change in the laws, he escaped the noose. In 1886, they sentenced him to forty years in prison instead. Local hunters testified that in the winter of 1874, where Packer and his party camped, plenty of game could be found. This confirmed that he lied when he claimed that wildlife could not be found, which is why he resorted to cannibalism. He purposely led the party astray. The local tribe offered a safe route for their travel, and warned them to wait until spring. He convinced them to disregard their advice.

After serving eighteen years at Canon City Penitentiary he got paroled in 1901. He died six years later at the age of sixty-seven. He suffered from dementia and upon his death; they cut his head off, dissected the brain and sold the skull to a traveling sideshow. No doubt, its attraction lay in the fact it belonged to the man who became known as the Colorado Cannibal.

VI. The Ghost in the Garden

ALBUQUERQUE, 1919. **The young novice leaned** against the kitchen door, and felt her heart pound in her chest. She crossed herself, and murmured all the prayers she knew like a litany, using the familiarity of the words to keep her anchored to the reality she recognized up to a few moments before.

Lightening flared inside amethyst-colored clouds, and the last rays of the sun dwindled beyond the horizon. Wind-driven rain attacked the windows, and the sound of thunder reverberated throughout the adobe house.

Sister Philomena steadied her breathing. Out of the darkness, a soft voice asked her, "What is it child? What is wrong?"

"Sister Magdalen, I hurried into the garden, making sure the shutters were fastened and the gates closed, and I thought I saw something," her voice stuttered, "I mean someone just standing in the shadow of the willow tree."

"Go on."

Sister Philomena continued in a suffocated whisper, "Sister, it looked like a woman, kneeling and weeping at the grave." She rushed on, "I know that Father Louis warns us against believing in superstitious things, but I couldn't help thinking of her." The novice stopped herself before naming what she feared she saw in the purple shadows of the garden.

"You mean La Llorona?"

"Yes, I saw her when lightening lit up the garden, and then I ran inside."

"Stoke up the fire, and let us sit in its warmth. We can eat soup and talk further." Sister Magdalen tapped a stick in front of her, finding a path in the darkened room to an area illuminated by the glowing embers in the hearth. The younger nun rushed forward, and guided her to a cushioned chair. Sister Magdalen barely sixty years old, had been losing her sight gradually, and now she could see nothing.

The novice clicked the light switch, and the bulb stayed dark. She lighted a few candles, and prepared their food. She looked over her shoulder at Sister Magdalen who sat in silence, apparently lost in thought.

The older nun said, "You did not see La Llorona. You thought I didn't believe you? I do, but the garden is not haunted by a ghost."

Sister Philomena, at a loss for words stared at the older nun. Sister Magdalen kind and peculiar, frequently made her feel she guarded many secrets. When assigned to help the older nun, the other novices whispered to her all the strange stories that were retold about the blind sister. She lived by herself in a small compound, not far from the convent attached to San Felipe Neri Church.

In 1881, she accompanied Sister Blandina to help build the convent for the Sisters of Charity. During these years, she joined the order leaving behind a tumultuous life. Though young, she had already endured something terrible because a jagged scar ringed her neck, and another stretched across her chest.

Sister Magdalen's one irrefutable talent lay in her ability to make things grow. She tended the gardens for the convent, and grew food served to the sisters. Later in a small house, enlarged to become where they sat now, she grew herbs. Many of them well known; others were rare.

Druggists everywhere came to buy these plants, stems and seeds from her. The money helped the sisters in their work among the poor. A Chinese lady visited her without fail throughout the years. She owned a laundry, and an apothecary shop in Chinatown.

A strange tale circulated about her as well. A few years ago, she set up a small apartment over one of her businesses. An old woman suffering from terrible rheumatism lived there. Two of the Chinese lady's daughters attended her until the day she died. The rumor whispered in town, said the Chinese lady called this Anglo woman, mother.

Sister Philomena came with a tray of food, and placed it in front of Sister Magdalen. The soup steamed aromatically, and a piece of bread she baked that morning completed the meal. They prayed over it, and the younger sister nibbled on a crust of bread. The fright she received drove all desire for food from her.

They sat in silence for a while, and then Sister Magdalen said, "You know that they placed you here not only to help me, but to be my apprentice as well. You have the magic in your hands that makes things grow."

Sister Philomena's mouth curved into an unconscious smile. "I am happy here learning from you."

"I know they told you stories about me before you came here. As your teacher I will allow you to ask me any questions you have, and I will answer them truthfully."

Sister Philomena pondered in silence what she should ask. Outside the wind howled around the edges of the one-story house, and before she could stop herself, she said, "About the man."

"Ah, the man buried in the garden?" The statement more than a question hung between them.

Sister Philomena licked her lips, ready for a rebuke as she continued, "Yes, he came here to die and yet they allowed him to stay that month with you, and even buried him on these grounds."

Sister Magdalen looked wistfully with her unseeing eyes into the fire. "Yes and such wonderful stories he told me in those few days. Of places and adventures; he fought many battles and truly, he was his brother's keeper."

"What did he battle?" Sister Philomena thought of the Great War. She leaned forward spreading her cold hands to the fire.

"Things I pray you never know of Sister Philomena," the older nun lowered her voice, being purposefully mysterious.

"Was he a monk or a priest? The only man who has ever visited you is Father Louis to hear your confession, and offer communion."

"No, neither, but he fought Evil as valiantly or more so than any man I know of."

Curiosity prompted the young nun to ask, "Why is it you have never left?" She hurried on before she lost her courage, "They even sent Sister Blandina back to Cincinnati. I have realized that Father Louis is nervous when he is here. He jumps at any noise, and he is always looking over his shoulder. When that man was here he never came, not even to anoint him and perform the last rites."

An intense, but secret expression crossed Sister Magdalen's face. "I have stayed here for my protection," she paused, "and to honor a debt. It is this agreement that allowed that man to stay here, and to rest where I can pray for him and plant beautiful flowers on his grave."

The wind outside picked up speed, rattling the windows and the rain thrummed like a war drum upon the glass, accompanied by a roll of thunder.

Sister Magdalen continued, "As to why Father Louis acts that way, I do not know, however heed my advice, do not ask him about this."

Many years before, Sister Magdalen took notice of how Father Louis asked about her. He wanted to know why she lived by herself in the small house with the walled courtyard, growing flowers, vegetables and herbs.

"Why didn't she live in the convent with the other sisters?" he asked. Like other priests before him, he felt genuine surprise when the diocese's bishop asked him to come by for a chat. The short, one-sided conversation ended when they told him to stop asking.

Sister Magdalen stifled a yawn, and stood up slowly, thereby ending the conversation. She took her walking stick, and told the young nun, "I will be at night prayers in my quarters. No need to accompany me." She left, tapping her way into the blue-black interior of the house.

The next day, darkness still lay on the land when Sister Philomena left to join the other nuns for Lauds. She returned when the sun peeked over the eastern horizon, and the small house smelled of fresh brewed coffee.

The young nun draped a long, white apron over her habit. She heard Sister Magdalen humming to herself in an adjacent workroom, as she inspected newly arrived flower bulbs. Sister Philomena grabbed a small basket from a hook by the door with plans to collect eggs, which were laid throughout the garden, by two itinerant hens she spent the day shooing away from the flowerbeds.

The rising sun illuminated the desert willow tree that grew in the middle of the garden. Droplets of water were still falling from its leaves. Her eyes traveled downward, and the basket slipped from her fingers. Wildflowers of different varieties covered the earth over the grave. Brown and barren only the day before, verbena, hyssop, primrose and snapdragon waved in the early morning breeze, their fragrance filling the air.

On the granite marker, the only words engraved were in Latin: *fidelis usque in sempiternum*, which translated to forever faithful; below it the years 1835 - 1919.

Sister Philomena realized in that moment that Sister Magdalen never explained who the lady she saw weeping over the grave was.

VII. Tears Dry

Present Day. EMA STOOD WATCHING THE fire being extinguished in slow degrees by the firemen. Dawn broke over the horizon as she returned to Slim's discarded pickup truck. She sat behind the wheel rehearsing in her mind what her next move would be. Plan B waited in the wings, and more, enough to span the length of the alphabet and beyond.

Ema calculated the storage unit she needed to access would not be open for another hour. Her belly grumbled with hunger, and she drove to a small family restaurant only a few blocks away. She slid into a stool at the counter, and ordered coffee and a homemade apple fritter. The low clacking of dishes sounded from the back, and a handful of people occupied the formica-topped tables. The low murmur of voices offered a sense of normalcy that Ema immersed herself in, knowing that this would be the last time she would visit this place.

A television hung on the wall, and Ema saw a young reporter standing in front of a smoldering mansion, which she called home until a few hours ago. The woman with a dramatic flair, explained the situation to her viewers tuning in for the morning news:

"The Topaz county Sheriff's Office reported a call came in about 5:20 a.m. Sunday morning for a structure fire at County

Highway 44 in the town of Vergo. Human remains were found after the fire was extinguished, according to a news release from the sheriff's office. The case is under investigation, but they do not suspect foul play at this time, according to the sheriff's office. An autopsy is scheduled and the cause of the fire is being investigated by the sheriff's office and the Topaz county Fire Investigation team. Sheriff's deputies, along with first responders from Vergo Fire/EMS and Fire District Alpha responded to the call."

Ema finished her meal, and left the money on the counter. She swiveled around on the stool, and looked across the room. Most of the people in the restaurant looked at her, but did not see her. Ema turned, and gazed at a small camera hanging in the corner. Angled to film the counter, the cooking area and the register by the door, a light blinked at its base. She stared hard at it, and the blinking stopped and it went dark. The owner would later realize it stopped working, and the film for that day had been corrupted.

Ema drove through mostly empty streets, passing saltbox houses many hung with autumn and thanksgiving decorations. Sunday gardeners raked falls leaves or washed their vehicles, happy in their ignorance that someone like her existed. They would find some of the creatures she battled in the pages of horror stories, which were considered strictly fiction.

The neighborhood changed as most of the houses lining the street stood abandoned. She turned down a short avenue, and left the truck parked. There were already two other vehicles down the street with broken windows and flat tires.

Ema walked the short distance to the storage place. A girl with blue hair, and a piercing in her eyebrow looked at her with a bored expression. Her face remained unchanged when Ema told her to close the account for the storage space. She popped her gum, took the payment and told Ema to make sure she took everything, or they would auction the items off. Ema noted two cameras angled towards the counter, but didn't even bother with them since they were fake.

Ema rolled up the door of the storage unit, and uncovered a sky blue, Thunderbird coupe that took up most of the space. She opened the trunk, and pulled out two bags. A duffle bag contained clothing, and a leather messenger bag had rolls of cash. The car turned over immediately, and she eased it slowly down the narrow passages of the storage park, until it emptied into the deserted street.

Ema headed toward the main highway that would take her south. She cruised by the street where Slim's truck already blended into the desolate feel of the area. She braked the car, and pulled it over to the curb to stare, not at the vehicle, but at the crow perched on the driver's side mirror. The bird issued a loud caw, ruffled its feathers and stared back at her. More than a hundred years evaporated in that moment when she recognized a Trezor underling hiding in the bird. This confirmed to her what she already suspected about the fire.

Like an experienced sailor who looks at the clouds, and the color of the sunset to determine if a storm is imminent, Ema recognized that prior to her encounter with Slim events were set in motion beyond her control. No doubt, the wheels of time were moving towards an important juxtaposition.

Ema understood that movement preserved life, and for years she hid out in this small town and others like it. Fear of dark spirits, demons or any being that crawled out of hell did not deter her. It still surprised her how many of them crossed her path, drawn like a moth to a flame. Her power had increased, but she felt emotionally detached from her human counterparts. She intentionally chose vessels that were so close to death, only the mechanics of keeping the body alive were left. Ema understood this placed her at a disadvantage, but after losing a human being who she bonded with, she suffered a deep sense of loss that took years to assuage. Mort's death affected her to a profound level.

She thought of the first time she saw him. He accompanied his older brother, and a small party headed to the goldfields of California. They stopped at a trading post owned by Alice, her avatar.

The Comanche kidnapped ten-year-old Alice from her family's farm. Left for dead on the banks of a rushing creek, she took Alice over when the perpetrator, a jealous woman in the tribe ambushed and drowned her. When Alice marched back into the camp with water still dripping from her clothes, the woman ran screaming to the tribe's medicine woman, and confessed her crime.

The medicine woman stared at Alice, known as Prairie Owl by the Comanche. She then told the chief that he must return the girl to her family, and that he must set out that very day. The chief knew by the woman's demeanor that he should not even ask the reason for her request. He quickly rounded up a small party of warriors, and set out before the sun disappeared beyond the horizon.

Throughout the years, many speculated how Alice lived by herself without being attacked by either the Comanche, or desperados who frequented the area. There were old-timers who commented how gunslingers infamous for killing without provocation, would unaccountably vanish. Their wanted posters hung in the sheriffs' office of the surrounding towns for years, the ends curled and frayed. No lawmen or bounty hunters came forward to claim the reward offered for their capture.

The day that Mort bought some supplies, none in the party suspected that they were incubating some type of contagion. They camped close to the trading post, and by the next morning, several in the party were running high fevers. Mort's brother died first, and there were few left to tend the sick. Alice, who lived alone caught the fever, and passed away in her bed in the small cabin where she lived.

The next day Ema saw when two of the men from the party took Mort, and dumped him by the side of a creek. They buried the first dead in a hastily dug, shallow trench. The second day, they didn't have the strength, or the desire to dig another pit. They felt death breathing on their own necks, and believed the boy would not live another day.

They were wrong; Morti still clung to life. Once she joined him, he pulled himself into the cool waters of the shallow creek, which lowered the high fever. Young and healthy, he responded immediately.

The next morning Ema used his body to return to the trading post. She freed the livestock, took Alice's horse and some supplies for the trip out west. Under loose floorboards, she retrieved a cache of coins that Alice had hoarded for the last twenty years. After this, she set fire to the place, including the woman's body that still lay in her bed.

Mort joined another group of miners and settlers who were heading to the trading post. They saw the smoke in the distance, and he warned them away with tales of fever and sickness. They needed no encouragement to put as much distance between themselves, and the column of black smoke that rose like a spiral into the air.

During those many miles on the Santa Fe Trail heading to California, Mort and she became acquainted. Ema explained what happened to him. She recognized the soul that dwelt in his body. Through countless lifetimes in the past, it accompanied her in a myriad of guises.

Ema blinked as the present intruded into her memories. She reminded herself this occurred over one hundred and fifty years ago. If ever a creature understood the immutable laws of time, it was she.

VIII. Ander

ANDER BELASKO SAT IN THE ELEVATED hunting blind and sighed. Complete darkness surrounded it, and he dozed on a padded chair with his feet propped up. What he hated about being out here by himself, is that it gave him too much time to think.

The day before a friend, and occasional business partner, Donny Figueroa called him unexpectedly. His hopes that he called with a job out of the country were quickly dashed. Instead, he ended up here.

Donny's company organized hunting and wildlife photography expeditions, and he hired Ander for his experience as an Army combat medic. Part of the services Donny provided included personnel who could handle medical emergencies in inhospitable terrain.

Donny, and Ander by extension as part of his team, worked with journalists, environmentalists, television and film producers, hunters and anyone that wanted to go into dangerous locations around the world.

When Donny asked him to scout out a location for someone who wanted to film ducks, and other waterfowl he guffawed into the phone. "This is a joke, right?" he asked Donny. It turned out it wasn't.

Ander lived in central Louisiana, not too far from the wildlife management park in question. Donny explained that a journalist and photographer on a time crunch, planned to be there only for the weekend. The timing couldn't have been better, since November saw the arrival of several species they expected to photograph. He wanted Ander to find a location with a clear line of sight to a body of water, and the surrounding habitat where the fowl congregated. Donny arranged for a blind to be set up ahead of time.

That's how he found himself cooling his heels out in the middle of nowhere. Ander estimated that it would be late in the day by the time he arrived, and most of the birds would be roosting. He planned to be there when the sun came up, and he could watch the activity of a marshy area not too far from the blind.

Upon his arrival, Ander scouted around the perimeter of a large pond. He disturbed a flock of herons and egrets that flew away, their wings catching the bluish red of the setting sun. Nearby, flies swarmed around a large mound that turned out to be the ravaged carcass of a shaggy, feral hog. It appeared to be dead less than twenty-four hours. Strange, he thought, a predator would have dragged it away from a watering hole. A searching wind prowled the woodland, far off a faint call echoed. He listened, but the sound faded.

Ander went back to the blind, and resigned himself to a boring night. He consoled himself with the thought of the easy money. However hours alone were not the solution when trying not to think about your crazy family, and how to avoid them for the holidays. He dreaded it. Donny usually did him a solid, and arranged to have work lined up during these months when nobody else wanted to work. This gave him a valid excuse to bow out, but this year his luck ran out.

Two of his older half-siblings lived in Oklahoma. He still failed to figure out why they were so insistent on including him in everything, if they were always mad at him. They weren't obvious about it, but an undercurrent of rage against him would manifest in a variety of ways. It got to the point, where he moved to a small town in Louisiana to put some distance from them.

He'd given the matter enough thought, and he understood the origins of it all commenced before his birth. His parents were older when they wed. Both of them were married before, with unhappy results. His mother had one twenty-year-old daughter, and his father a teenage son who lived with his ex-wife.

His sister eloped and married the laziest man she found, good-looking but bone idle. His brother continued living with his mother who still railed against his father, even though they parted ways many years before.

Ander thought his parent's marriage made him believe in soul mates. From the moment they met, they had eyes only for each other. They became the best version of themselves within their marriage. Contrary to what many people believed, his parents set out to conceive him. Many considered his mother too old at the age of forty to have another child, and his father raised eyebrows when he became a father at the age of fifty-two. Wouldn't he be happier waiting for grandchildren? They both knew these whispers circulated among friends and family. They didn't care.

To say they lavished him with love would be an understatement. His father had inherited the small home they lived in, so his mother had no need to work and cared for him until he started grade school. His father gave him not only love, but also his time. This included helping him with homework, and weekend trips to fish and hunt. They gave him boundaries, and taught him responsibility. He learned the value of persisting when he failed, and how to master something through practice.

He remembered hearing his mother humming while she cooked. Toys were spread out around the kitchen, practically under her feet, but she never scolded him. Instead, she would just step over the little boy as he played. His fondest memories were of succulent aromas filling the air, and his mother sitting at the kitchen table chatting with a neighbor while they drank a cup of coffee.

Her good friends wouldn't even come to the front door; they came to the screen door on the side of the house that led to the kitchen, and call out her name. A large tree shaded the area, and a cool breeze would waft into the room in the summer.

His brother and sister visited, and as he grew older, he recognized that they looked at him with hostile eyes. Each of them would be mad at their respective parent, and out-and-out hated their spouse.

Both of his parents did everything in their power to bridge the gulf of enmity that grew between them and their children, but to no avail. If anything, the love and happiness that encapsulated their household exacerbated every negative suspicion they fostered. Their visits became more seldom as time went by.

Ander finished a two-year stint at a community college where he studied to become a paramedic, with plans to join a fire department, but everything changed the day his mother died. He remembered arriving at home to find his father holding the phone, with a look on his face that turned his blood to ice. He feared something terrible occurred. His father just kept repeating, "Your mother, your mother."

Ander took the phone from his father, and a man's voice directed him to go to the hospital. The manager of the local supermarket told him his mother collapsed while shopping, and paramedics were transporting her to the emergency room. As a friend of the family, he wanted to let them know what happened to her.

By the time they reached the hospital, the medical team had already started to work on his mother, but the doctor that came out to see them looked grim. His mother suffered a cerebral hemorrhage. Later that night the doctor confirmed that only machinery kept her alive, and her brain had stopped functioning.

His father gave him the task of signing the paperwork to remove her from everything that sustained her life. His father, seventy-five years old, alert and full of vitality until then, became a shriveled and absent-minded old man in twenty-four hours. He willed himself to die two years later.

After his father's funeral, he realized that he needed time and distance away from his siblings. They were not capable of giving him the comfort he yearned for as he mourned his parents.

The day of his father's burial, neighbors, friends from church and a smattering of distant relatives filled the small house. He stood by himself when his brother came up to him. He brought up the subject that the house belonged to the Belasko family. Why didn't he have any rights to it? Ander did not say a word and just eyed him up and down, and that ended that conversation for the time being.

Ander retreated to the kitchen where his sister found him. She asked him about the life insurance money their mother left. When he stared at her without saying a word, she said in a wheedling voice if he would let her stay in the house with her husband and kids. She pointed out that now he had all this extra space. Her husband needed a job and would get one soon, but in the meantime could they move in? She smiled, and looked at him with cold eyes that reminded him of a shark.

A week later, the family attorney read his father's will, which left everything to Ander. His siblings called him that night, and he did not even bother to answer the phone. Instead, he contacted a friend who recommended a real estate agent, who happened to be his mother and would go the extra mile for him.

She came to see him the next day, and he explained to her that he wanted to sell the house. The structure small and old had been lovingly tended by his father, who had been an excellent handyman. It sat on five acres of land. She assured him it would sell in a short amount of time, and probably over the asking price.

The following weekend he held an estate sale. With the exception of a few personal items that belonged to his parents and the appliances, he put everything inside the home up for sale. The unsold items he donated to the local church his parents attended. A sleeping bag on the floor served as his bed. The calls from his siblings continued, and he still kept hitting the ignore button on his phone when he saw their name light up the display.

The only thing he understood amidst the heartache that engulfed him is neither of them would ever set foot, much less live inside the wonderful place that sheltered his parents in their happiest years. His most precious memories were set against the backdrop of this home.

Two weeks later the real estate agent called with a contract from very interested buyers. They wanted to close right away since they were moving in from out of state. The following day he stopped at an Army recruiting office. Ander told them about his education, and that he wanted to be a medic. He walked out knowing that he would soon be shipped out for basic training.

The day after the sale of the house, he told his attorney to split the proceeds three ways. His instructions were to wait until he left to boot camp, then to send his brother and sister their portion of the money. Under no circumstance were they to know of his whereabouts.

Thirteen years later, he found himself sitting inside a hunting blind trying to figure out how he could avoid seeing them for Thanksgiving.

Ander looked at his phone, and guessed in another hour the sun would be coming up. He leaned his head back when a sound brought him to his feet. Something rustled the leaves under the blind. It sounded like a large animal, possibly a bear. Suddenly a disgusting odor drifted up through the trap door. Pungent and stinking of animal urine, the musky smell reminded him of an animal's lair. He felt engulfed by the total silence that descended on the area.

Ander remembered the dead hog, yet he suspected the carcass did not cause the stench. He went to put his hand on the Beretta M-9 he clipped on his belt earlier that day, and his hand found nothing. He realized then that he left it in his truck's glove compartment. He removed it when he walked into a fast-food restaurant to get something to eat on his way up here.

A thick fog blanketed the area. A door leading to a ladder below the blind provided the only exit. He opened it, and saw the swirling mist and nothing else. The nauseating odor left no doubt the animal could only be a few feet away. Ander knew bears didn't smell like this. Hell, no animals he knew of smelled like this. Whatever lurked in the brush, he could not face it unarmed. However to reach the truck he had to run through low-lying fog that obscured the ground.

The odor lessened a bit, and he climbed down the ladder with slow steps; scanning all around him, straining his eyes, but saw nothing. He gripped his car keys in one hand, and stood there undecided whether to stay or go. From across the large pond a howl echoed. It thrummed in the silence of the marshy swamp area. In that moment, Ander realized the blind offered no protection from whatever made that call. He could not remember ever hearing a cry like that.

He might not get another chance to know where this thing stood, so he took off running towards the trail leading to his vehicle. Despite the cool air, he felt sweat break out all over his body as he ran full tilt in the darkness, relying on memory to stay on the path. He put his head down, and his arms pumped; the odor of fear trailing behind him like a ribbon.

First, he heard his shoes crunching on the small rocks, and his heavy breathing. Somewhere in the boggy area, a loon called out. Then the wail sounded behind him, reverberating in a way that let him know that it trailed close on his heels. Upon rounding a curve in the trail, he clicked the key fob. The truck's headlights came on, and it gave him a clear marker where sanctuary lay. Then the animal roared again, and he heard the brush breaking as whatever pursued him picked up the pace, trying to head him off before he made it to the truck.

Coming up on the passenger door, he transferred the fob to his left hand, and put every ounce of speed left in his body with the hope of gaining a few second in which to open the door. The thing bellowed once more, and he heard the gravel spatter behind him as it moved from the trees to the trail. With his right hand, he reached out and with a fluid movement that he attributed to the adrenaline pumping in his body, opened the truck door, slid in and slammed it behind him.

A few seconds afterwards, his pursuer collided into the truck door rocking the entire vehicle. He listened to the crunch of metal as the door buckled in. He looked over his shoulder, and saw something unbelievable. A wolf-like creature stared at him with red eyes, its breath fogging the glass as it panted, revealing long fangs. Pointed ears and a long muzzle dominated its face. It pressed a dog-like hand with an opposable thumb on the window. Long claws tipped the end of each digit.

Ander pressed the button on the fob to lock the doors. His eyes met with that of the creature that looked at him with preternatural intelligence. Thick black fur covered its wide, muscled torso. He saw it crouched over to look into the window at him. The thing stood on its hind legs, and his brain tried to make sense of what he saw slavering and staring at him through a piece of glass.

Ander's body, slick with the sour sweat of fear trembled. He kept staring at the thing while he opened the glove compartment, and drew out his gun. Its eyes followed his movement as he withdrew the firearm. Then the creature threw its head back, and shrieked a shrill inhuman cry. At that moment, he gave up all thought of confrontation, and scrambled behind the steering wheel and turned the truck on. He threw the pick-up into reverse and floored it. The creature vanished from the window, and as he braked to change direction, he listened to a thump in the truck's bed. He didn't even bother to see what made the truck bounce, because it could only be one thing.

Ander's thoughts spun in all direction. He breathed harshly and his eyes tracked the headlights as they cut through the swirling mist. He tried to keep the truck on the narrow road, aware that beyond it the terrain sloped downwards into marshy swampland.

He listened to the animal issue a deep growl, before a loud crash sounded on the roof of the truck. More thumps followed, and then Ander flinched when the crack of the window shattering filled the cab of the pick-up. He felt a rush of cold air pour in.

Ander realized he needed to get off the trail, and onto the main highway so he could pick up speed. He pressed down on the accelerator as he saw the entrance to the two-lane road coming up ahead. The thoroughfare didn't have heavy traffic, and he hoped that at this early hour, it would be desolate, but he also knew eighteen-wheelers traversing Louisiana favored this route.

He pressed hard on the accelerator when the glass behind him splintered further, and the sound of the creature trying to wedge its body in through the opening screeched in the silence of the cab. The truck became airborne as the tires hit the lip of the road, and at that same instant, something sharp raked the edge of his right shoulder. Out of his peripheral vision, Ander saw the bright glare of headlights and the screech of tires. He pulled hard on the steering wheel to stop the truck from crossing over the highway, and running into large trees on the other side of the asphalt. Then the sickening sensation of the truck as it rolled over caused him to lose all sense of direction.

He didn't have his seat belt on, and he clung onto the steering wheel with all his strength. The lower part of his body went everywhere, and the airbags punched him in the face and chest. Ander lost consciousness for a moment, and when he came to, he found his body wedged inside the cab. The truck sat pinned against the thick trunks of pine trees. A detached section of his mind estimated that first responders would have to use the Jaws of Life to extract him.

A scratching noise sounded outside, and then a long-fingered, furry hand came through the opening where the back window had been knocked out. Trapped, Ander waited for someone to wake him from the horrible nightmare.

The tang of gasoline filled the air, and the clawed hand withdrew. A small lick of flame burst from the area of the engine, and Ander struggled to dislodge his bruised body. He saw the fire increase, and he feared that in a moment he would die burned to death inside the truck. Even if emergency services were racing to him, they would arrive too late. He coughed as fumes and smoke filled the inside of the cramped space. His eyes watered, and they could not stay open. The heat increased, and Ander feared losing consciousness but he could not prevent it. From somewhere far away he listened to the crackle of fire, and then a high-pitched whimper. The scream of tortured metal followed it, and then the pressure around his body eased. Soft hands touched his face, and then his neck, searching for a pulse.

Ander's felt his body pulled out with care, and then stretched out on his back. With a strange hypersensitivity, he felt rocks under him poking through his clothing. The sweet, cool redolence of pre-dawn air filled his nostrils, and he heard the distant sound of sirens.

He opened his eyes, and saw a beautiful face staring down at him. Above her, tall trees stretched up into the indigo sky. He looked around for other people, the ones who saved his life and his eyes returned to the only one there.

She whispered words to him that eased his fear, "You are safe."

Ander experienced a blessed relief, as his consciousness slipped. However as he drifted off, he recognized that his body picked itself up, but a part of his brain did not recognize giving these commands to his extremities.

A person watching would have seen a muscled young man, with disheveled and torn clothing walk towards a light blue vehicle parked on the side of the road. He bled from his face and hands as he slid behind the steering wheel of the idling car. It pulled off into the deserted road, and traveled away at a regular speed.

A few seconds later, a fire engine rolled up with police vehicles behind it; blue and red lights illuminating the large trees that lined the two-lane highway. Before any of the personnel disembarked, the truck exploded into a fireball.

IX. He Smiled Fierce

A CAR FROM THE D'ETCHEPARE POLICE department rolled up the long driveway to a whitewashed bungalow with a verandah that stretched across the front of the house. Two large cypress trees with Spanish moss hanging from its branches shaded the walkway

A man exited the house before the car came to a complete stop. He stood watching with an impassive expression, as a young officer mounted three steps to stand beside him. A long gash across his forehead marred the lean hardness of his triangular face, and high cheekbones. Cropped close to the skull, his bright red hair set off green eyes that contrasted his dark skin. This, and his muscular build testified that he spent a great deal of time outdoors.

"Ander Belasko?"

"Yes."

"I'm sure you know why I'm here. Your truck has been recovered after being involved in a serious accident. We didn't know if you drove it, or if someone stole it. It looks like you were behind the wheel."

"Yes, a passing motorist helped me out. They intended to take me to a hospital, but I knew I didn't need to go over some bumps and bruises. I planned on calling your department today."

"Mr. Belasko, this is your case number," he handed over a card, "and that is the tow yard where the vehicle is being stored at." He glanced down at Ander's bruised hands, "How did the accident occur?"

"I exited onto the road and a car speeding down the highway without its headlights on, almost t-boned me. I turned too sharply trying to avoid hitting it, and the truck started to roll."

"Do you remember anything about the other vehicle?"

"No I don't. I lost control of the truck, and they didn't stop."

"You can pick up a copy of your report in a week. Good luck to you."

Ander observed the car as it drove away. He could tell the officer had not seen what his truck looked like; otherwise, he would have found it hard to believe that anyone inside of it got out alive.

The house's cool darkness welcomed Ander back inside. He looked out the back window, and saw the blue thunderbird parked behind the house. He turned away, and went to his bedroom where he laid down on the bed. His limbs went limp; a mauve shimmering outlined his form and then next to him Ema's naked body stretched out. Her eggshell blue tinted skin glistened with moisture.

She stood up next to the bed; her complexion had turned a rosy pink. She contemplated the man as he slept, noticing his deep and even breathing. There were no broken bones or internal injuries, and sleep assured his recovery.

Nightfall engulfed the verandah in darkness when Donny Figueroa knocked on the front door of Ander's house. He looked with curious eyes everywhere, since he had never come to the property before. After trying to speak to him all day without success, he didn't know what else to do. Ander, unquestionably reliable also valued his privacy, but he needed to know what happened.

Donny didn't see his truck parked in the driveway, and turned to leave when the porch light went on. As the door opened, he said in a concerned voice, "Ander, why haven't you..." he stopped in mid-sentence when he saw who stood framed in the entryway.

A tall woman with a long braid hanging over her shoulder stared at him. She looked to be in her mid-thirties, and in the full bloom of womanhood. The fullness of her figure made him think she already gave birth to children. Dressed in jeans and a pink tank top, he knew that if she walked into a room, every head would turn to look at her, especially the men. How did Ander keep her a secret?

He stuttered like an adolescent, "I'm... I'm sorry I thought you were Ander. Is he home?"

She stepped back inside the house. "Yes he is, but something happened."

Donny stood looking at her. "Something happened? Is he okay? I've tried to reach him all day long on his phone."

"He's unharmed, but he did have an accident."

"I knew something went wrong." The middle-aged man said in an alarmed voice.

Ema cocked her head to one side, and looked at him. He had dark hair salted with gray and arrogant eyes. She said quietly, "I can tell you more about it."

"Yeah, that would be great."

Silence fell between them, and then Ema smiled at him faintly and said, "Forgive my manners, please come inside and take a seat."

Donny wiped his feet on the welcome mat bordered with sunflowers and stepped inside. Ander furnished the house in modern-male-hardly-ever-home style. The rustic furniture made of wood held deep, comfortable cushions. Neutral-colored decorations adorned the space, and the refrigerator-white walls were naked. A large, lavender candle that burned on the coffee table provided the only feminine touch.

Donny sat down, and he looked at the woman curled on the sofa across from him. The lamplight reflected on the burnished red of her hair. Her face was thin with dark brows that arched over sloe eyes rimmed with long lashes. Her nose belonged on a Grecian statue. The expressive mouth with a full lower lip begged a kiss, he thought. The totality was an arresting, and exotic look.

Donny cleared his throat, "What happened?"

"The accident occurred at a hunting preserve not too far from here. The other driver fled the scene. Ander is okay. I can't say the same for the truck."

"A photography shoot is scheduled for this weekend, and he went to scout the location for me." Donny paused, "My name is Donny, I've been working with Ander for a few years.

I don't know if he's mentioned my name." His voice trailed off.

"Yes he has."

An awkward silence fell between them once again, and Donny thought how strange to have a beautiful woman who spoke so little, especially about herself.

"Umm, I'm sorry but what's your name?"

Ema smiled enigmatically at him and said, "You can call me Em."

"Em, can I speak to Ander?"

"Donny he's sleeping because he got bruised up and needs his rest, but I will let him know you came by when he wakes up."

"Yes, well tell him to call me when he has a chance."

"It will take a few days because he has to replace his phone."

Donny stood up, and Ema walked him to the door. She felt he waited only for one comment from her to continue the conversation and satisfy his curiosity, but she didn't offer him the opening.

Once Donny stood outside, she waved at him and closed the door, leaving him to walk to his car. He wondered how soon he could get answers to the questions that swirled in his mind about this woman.

Ema went to the bedroom, and sat down next to Ander. She placed some pain relievers and a bottle of water on the nightstand. She brushed the wound on his forehead with gentle fingers. His eyes fluttered open.

"Ema." his voice croaked.

She smiled, and helped him sit up. He groaned as pain shot through his body. She offered him the pills, and the bottle of water. He drank thirstily and then looked at her, studying her face, and he reached out and touched the thick braid that fell across her shoulder. This woman had saved him.

From the moment that Ema joined him, their spirits conversed and meshed. Ander's subconscious recognized everything about her, and his conscious mind needed time to catch up. However, already recognition and a sense of comfort emanated from her.

Ema told him that Donny came by to see him. He grimaced and said, "I'll call him in a few days, and let him know I won't be able to take any jobs for a while."

Ema chuckled, "He was shocked to see me."

"I bet he was. We've worked together for a few years, but even though I keep a low profile on my personal life, I've never mentioned an Ema being in the picture."

"He barely contained his curiosity."

"I'm not surprised. Donny always mixes business and pleasure, and even though he's not a sailor, you know that saying about a girl in every port, that's his mantra. I think that's part of the reason he has so many clients."

Ander shifted on the bed and his face tightened with the soreness that throbbed across his torso. He eased back on the pillow.

"Ema, I want to ask you about what chased me. I know I saw it with my own eyes, but I still can't understand it."

"Ander we will talk about that and more in the coming days, but the most important thing is for you to rest and recover from your injuries. I am here and watching over you."

Ander smiled at her. He caught her hand in his and whispered, "Thank you."

X. The Early Bird Gets the Worm

KILL, THE ONLY THING KYLE EARL KOSHEEN knew how to do well besides drive a truck. The Army booted him out in 1972 with a dishonorable discharge. After abusing and abandoning his wife and two children in California, he took up trucking. Life on the road suited his sadistic ways.

Kosheen kept to himself, and those who met him soon realized his mind existed perpetually in a dark place. Even proprietors of brothels and S&M clubs, used to bizarre behavior, were uncomfortable with the aura of uncontained menace exuding from him.

In between stops at disreputable establishments, he would pick up women at truck stops or along trucker-heavy locations. He would rape then torture them. The first time he killed a hitchhiker he abducted, he knew he would never deny himself the euphoria that flooded his being.

Other truckers recognized his sleeper cab truck by a prominent Earl-E Trucking written in cursive gold lettering across the eighteen-wheeler's door. To keep his victims close he converted it into a torture chamber. His tools of choice were whips and chains. Some victims he killed right away, others he kept with him for over a week, discarding their bodies off different highways in the United States.

During the 1980s, they charged him with a case of sexual assault, and another time unlawful imprisonment. However, the cases were dismissed when the accusers refused to testify against him.

Kosheen's takeaway from these encounters with the law amounted to being more careful, and not to leave any witnesses behind. These lessons served him well; now in his late sixties he evaded being arrested again.

He headed towards Texas to visit a swinger's bar recommended by the underground network he belonged to, however the true visit to the area hinged on a phone call. The caller owned a bondage club with a job that guaranteed triple his normal fee. He mentally rubbed his hands together, because he knew that special packages usually contained humans.

Kosheen stared out the windshield of the truck, his pasty face illuminated by the green glow of the dashboard. He belched the taste of the greasy chicken he ate at the last stop he made. He didn't have a trailer attached, and the semi sped through the night, traveling in a southwest direction through Louisiana.

Off to his left he read the signage of a wildlife management area, and then the proverbial light bulb went off in his head. He couldn't think of a better place to rid himself of a package sitting behind his seat. The only one left.

Kosheen pulled off the road, and switched on the truck's blinkers. He inspected the area, and noted a blackened section near the trees where the scorched vegetation indicated a recent fire. He reached into a red cooler, and pulled out something about the size of a small ham wrapped in plastic. Blood pooled in pockets inside of it. The head of a teenage boy he killed two days before stared at him with sightless eyes through the thick, clear membrane. The other body parts littered the highway en route to his destination in Texas.

He checked the road for the glow of other headlights, and with a grunt climbed down from the truck. He meandered towards an area where the trees grew the thickest. In the act of heaving the package out into the woodland, twigs snapped and a doe bounded towards him brushing close enough that he could have touched it. He first thought it ran from a predator. Then an odor hit him that made his eyes water. He knew the stink of rotting meat, and this is what wafted in the animal's wake. The deer crossed the road, and passed from sight into the wilderness beyond.

Kosheen turned, and tried to ascend the incline to where his truck idled. His boots kept slipping on the dew-laden grass, and then he made out a raspy growl full of phlegm coming from behind him. He lacked the imagination to conjure what made that noise, so he found himself turning around to face it. His eyes widened, and he experienced what he caused so many times to his victims, which was the inability to scream because of fright.

In the yellow pool of illumination coming from the headlights, he saw a tall figure covered in black fur that moved in the slight breeze. Dried blood covered its torso. It looked like a wolf, but its lower jaw had been torn away, and the long, purple tongue lolled down filled with a yellowish froth. One eye flickered with an orange light and in place of the other one a round, bloody cavern held an eyeball by a string of flesh. It stood teetering on its two hind legs, but one forearm dangled, held only by a flap of skin, and it could not maintain its equilibrium. The bouquet of putrefaction came from it in waves. It fell forward to stand on three legs, and its breath sounded horribly audible and full of mucus.

Kosheen kept his eyes locked on it and walked backwards, concentrating on keeping his feet under him. Without warning, the thing scuttled forward knocking the man down and lying on top of him like a lover. Kosheen opened his mouth, and released the scream locked inside of him. The thing placed its bloody snout inside his gaping mouth, muffling all sound. The sick effluvium filled his nostrils. A thick, viscous liquid poured down his throat, and it continued despite his attempts to vomit.

Kosheen listened to something whisper in his mind, "I am with you."

An intense pain flooded every nerve in his body, and he thought this must be what electrocution felt like. He pissed and shit on himself. The animal grew still, and he pushed the weight of it off his chest. He leaned on his elbow to expel vomit, which projected from his mouth in an arch.

Kosheen looked askance at the thing that draped over him, and he realized it no longer lived. He pushed against its chest and his hand sank into putrid flesh. He inched out from underneath it, and stood on legs that trembled and jerked.

Kosheen stripped off all his clothing, including his boots, and left the items scattered on top of the rotting carcass. He walked back to the truck and rummaged for clean clothing from a pile he tossed in the corner of the cab.

The trucker steered the semi back on the road, and then made a u-turn. He parked it on the grassy shoulder by the trail that led into the wildlife preserve. Unerringly he followed the trail that led to the deserted hunter's blind. Once inside, he licked a discarded coffee cup left by Ander. On the floor, he found a baseball cap; he smelled it and then stuffed it in his back pocket.

A few minutes later, back in his truck, he looked across the road and saw two, tall wolfish-looking figures pulling the dead body between them back into the woods.

Once on the road he headed for the nearest truck stop where he slept. His body cried out for rest, and nausea roiled his gut. Kosheen didn't understand what had gone wrong, however he knew one thing, any thought of heading to Texas receded into a pinpoint of nothingness. Something close by required his undivided attention.

XI. No Peace for the Wicked

SLEEP FLED, AND EMA WAITED A MOMENT before opening her eyes. She sensed a shift. Next to her Ander breathed deeply with an occasional soft snore. She touched his forehead, checking for fever and his skin felt cool.

She walked in the murkiness to a large picture window that overlooked the area behind the house. Her car silvered by the moonlight gleamed in the stillness of the night, and beyond it, a large shed swathed in confederate jasmine stood sentinel. The ten-acre property had only twelve thousand feet around the house cleared. Undeveloped woodland and marshes stretched off into the horizon.

Ander's property sat on the outskirts of the town of D'Etchepare. Settled in 1765 by the French; in 1807 they officially founded the town, and life and history unfolded at its leisure. The remoteness of the place is what convinced Ander to purchase the property.

Ema stared into the inky penumbra of the forest, where she saw more than one tall figure move under the cypress trees. A sickle moon slipped between the clouds overhead, and the cool air fragranced with the spice of damp earth hung still in expectation. Somewhere close by a great horned owl hooted out a courtship call.

She stepped onto a tiled area outside the rear door of the house. A gazebo stood stoic and tolerant of the elements; old paint scaled from the wooden posts holding up its roof. Ema walked on bare feet to stand underneath it.

There she understood the nuances of their desire. They communicated not in words, but in simple and eloquent symbols.

She looked over her shoulder and flicked her forefinger in the house's direction. A small blue cube flew, growing as it twirled through space. It intensified to a neon hue and outlined a tall, broad-shouldered human figure that held a spear. In contrast, its doglike head ended with tall pointed ears and a delicate snout. It bowed in obeisance to Ema, and faded into the wall of the structure.

The tall woman walked down a path, laid out by rough-hewn garden stones that ended at the tree line. She kept walking, watching three wolf-like figures circle around her. They did not disguise their movement, and twigs snapped and branches shook in their wake. She caught the scent of their animal tang mingled with the fecundity of living in the natural world. She came to a clearing that glimmered in the moonlight, and waited.

One figure rose on its hind legs, and approached Ema. The alpha female stood over seven feet in height. She had a thick coat the color of ochre. She yipped and snarled, and as the woman waved her hand, the growls turned into words.

"Sibyllina, I come to pay my debt to you. You heeded my call when I came to you in dreamtime, and set my mate free from the dark one who took him over. You rent his flesh and fur so none could use it."

The animal's eyes glimmered with an orange light in the oblique darkness. She fell forward and stood on all four legs. The creature padded forward until she stood before Ema. She sat on her haunches, and her muzzle level with the woman's face displayed sharp fangs. She spoke with bitterness, "I have no mate, and I will take my offspring away from this place."

Ema's voice held an infinitely compassionate tone, "You are wise to do so; there is a dangerous turbulence that has pervaded these woods."

"Before I leave, I will tell you that the corruption that chased away my mate's spirit reanimated his corpse for a few moments, before it jumped into a man. He stopped there to throw away the head of another human."

Ema's brow lifted in consternation, "A human head?"

The creature continued in a harsh, raw voice, "He stank of death and blood. He hunts and kills humans; many of them. He left in the machinery that thunders down the strip where nothing grows."

Ema's voice though quiet, carried an ominous quality. "Your debt is more than paid."

The animal raised its snout to the air, savoring the chilled breeze as it wafted through the copse of trees, and it continued in its guttural voice, "It went to seek the scent of the man you saved. It is hunting this human." The clarity of her words faded, and turned into low growls.

Ema stepped forward and asked, "Will you permit me?"

The animal stilled, and Ema passed her hands through the thick fur around her neck. It in turn sniffed Ema's midsection. It turned and trotted off into the darkness, the other two figures following close behind it.

The morning sun slanted into the kitchen. Ander sat on a chair with a steaming cup of coffee in front of him. He wore boxer shorts and a well-washed sweatshirt. Reddish stubble contoured his face. He said in a dull and troubled voice, "When I was a kid my parents told me there were no such things as monsters. Were they liars? To think I was afraid of a dark closet."

Ema leaned backwards against the kitchen counter listening to him. She made use of his garments, and wore a pair of baby blue boxer shorts and a white t-shirt. Her dark auburn hair hung loose to her waist.

"There are many nasty things, most of them beyond what most humans can imagine. What pursued you is not the worse. Simply an animal taken over by a dangerous being. I don't want to cloud your judgment Ander by what I'm telling you, but it is best you know that much of what you understand as reality, is only a facade."

Ander looked at her with earnest eyes, "I am not accustomed to feeling such fear. I always thought when a person became this frightened they based it on something fictional; anything but reality."

Ema paused a moment, pondering how to explain to him the narrowness created by his five senses. "The universe and all its dimensions is always in flux, trying to maintain harmony and balance; it is war and peace. That is the natural order of things, however there are beings that are bitter and want to wage a war within a war without the benefit of rules. There is no place for them in this order, even within the disorder of chaos. They have a blood feud with all living things, and they exist in a vicious circle of destruction."

A long, brittle silence came between them. Ema understood better than he realized how difficult this new reality could be to accept. He now existed in a world where no quarter was asked for, and none was given. The creatures that existed there felt an unquenchable enmity, and hatred that human beings found difficult to accept. She understood that no explanation would suffice, and that in time he would learn this lesson.

Ander stared into Ema's eyes, leaned forward and lowered his voice when he asked her, "Are you human?"

Her left eyebrow raised a fraction, "Yes Ander I am, and I am not immortal."

"Then how do you exist?"

Ema thought of the many times she held this conversation, but always tailored to the person who asked it, and the moment in history they lived in.

"There are *some* laws of physics that roughly say *certain* things can't occupy the same space at the same time. However, I can vibrate at a different speed thus allowing me to be in you, and with you. As more time passes, you will understand better."

His mouth became tight and grim, "What now Ema?"

She sighed knowing there would be time enough later to explain, and teach him what existed in the light and tenebrosity of the world he now lived in.

"You are being hunted by a man. The creature that possessed what attacked you has now moved on to another human being; an evil human. This is a dangerous pairing. But the more I think about it, it is the very nature of evil that we will use to our advantage."

Ander blinked at her in silence. He didn't anticipate this answer. A part of him realized that his expectations were bound to be shattered, but not so soon. Her next words confirmed this.

"Are you ready to be bait?"

"Will we kill what chased me?"

"In a manner of speaking, yes."

"Then, fuck yeah."

He grunted in pain as he stood up and straightened out. He walked down the hallway towards his bedroom. Then he stopped, turned around and with a quizzical look on his face said, "Ema, you know that when you pulled me from the truck, and I saw your face and heard your voice, I had a déjà vu moment. I thought I recognized you. You must think I'm a real pussy for believing that sappy shit."

"No Ander, not at all," she replied with a smile.

XII. Breathe In

FALL BROUGHT ITS GILDED TINT to the landscape, and Ander contemplated his reflection from the back seat of the Uber car taking him to the car rental agency. He realized that he would measure the rest of his life, based on his experiences of the last twenty-four hours.

Earlier he spent a few minutes at his computer, and reported the accident. He checked his email to discover that Donny sent him numerous messages, even after stopping at the house. Amidst the multiple offers for any help, obviously he desired to speak to him one-on-one. Donny never struck him as an overly curious guy, but now it appeared he couldn't wait to find out what happened. He replied with a short message, asking to be put on a back burner for any new jobs.

Ander eyed a fire engine red pickup parked in the rental agency's lot, and remembered his role as demon bait when he asked for it. A few minutes later, he drove down the street reveling in the new car smell. Before arriving at the Lunch Car Cafeteria, his replacement phone sat on the seat next to him. The eatery had fed the residents of D'Etchepare for the last forty years, and being open twenty-four hours it became a favorite spot for the local police. Now, he saw several cruisers parked in front of the restaurant, and when he walked in, several called out to him.

Patsy Cline's *I Fall to Pieces* played through several speakers in the diner. A thickset man with a bullet head and short-cropped hair waved him over to the counter where he sat. Jamie Warrensburg, better known as War had been Ander's friend for several years. A few years older than Ander, his twenty-year anniversary with the department had just passed.

He pointed to the empty seat next to him, and gave Ander a hearty handshake. When the younger man winced in pain, he stopped and apologized.

"Fuck sorry Ander. I was about to say you look great for a guy that escaped a truck that blew up."

"Yeah well that's what happens, when you bounce around the inside holding on to the steering wheel, thinking any moment it will break off in your hands."

War grunted and turned back to slurp from his soft drink; he commented, "Well you're one lucky son of a bitch."

The waitress stopped in front of Ander who ordered a club sandwich and a chocolate shake. He eyed War's almost empty plate, and asked Mindy the waitress about their homemade apple pie.

"We have some, but it's going fast." She replied.

"War, why don't you get a slice on me? I've been going stir crazy in my house, and would appreciate some company."

"Turn down a slice of apple pie? Hell no, hey Mindy slap some vanilla ice cream on mine."

Mindy gave him a thumbs-up as she walked away and passed the order over to the cook.

Chatter flowed around them, and ceiling fans twirled overhead. A bell over the door would chime when someone arrived or left.

Ander shared some stories with War about his last trip, and then asked him about any crazy calls he received. The conversation stopped when Mindy served Ander his food. She placed a steaming slice of apple pie with a melting ball of ice cream in front of War.

The stocky man threw back his head and chuckled, "Man, strange you should ask about that. Just last night I went to one that was a first for me."

"Yeah, what happened?"

"You know that mobile home park, right next to the truck stop, off the highway?"

"Sure."

"Well there's an old gal named Butters who lives in this rickety single-wide that I think dates back to 1970. She's known for picking up strays at the truck stop. Over the years, we've gotten calls when she and her newest boyfriend were drunk and argued. When I heard the address for a DV incident I volunteered to take the call, because I knew it could be only one person."

Ander stayed quiet, not wanting to interrupt his story.

War cleared his throat and his demeanor grew more serious, "Ander when I got out there, this woman is waiting for me outside. Her neighbor from next door is hugging her, and Butters is shaking like she's got Parkinson's. I've seen people who are scared, and I will tell you this woman looked

WALKER BETWEEN THE WORLDS

terrified. It took a bit to calm her down so she could explain what happened."

Ander realized he hit pay dirt on his first attempt. He listened to War with rapt attention.

"Like most of her stories, it starts out when she brings somebody home. She's planning to have a few drinks, smoke some weed and at her age fall asleep before getting to the big nasty. She said she went to the bathroom, and when she's finishing up, she heard two people arguing in the living room. One voice she recognizes as the guy she picked up, the other one is unknown."

War paused, and then his face went grim. "Butters is crazy, but not stupid. She waits inside the bathroom, thinking this guy got followed to her place. At this point, all she wants to do is kick herself for bringing this guy home."

Ander interjected, "That honeymoon ended quick."

War chuckled and continued, "She said that the voices changed, and described it as screaming and growling. She even thought someone brought a dog inside the trailer. Then they're using a language she can't understand. Once Butters heard something break, she runs out thinking they're going to trash her place. This is where her story goes into the twilight zone territory. The first thing that hits her is a smell like a sewer broke, then she sees this guy she picked up wrestling with another guy who's growing out of his side. They have each other by the neck, because they're trying to bite one another."

War stopped, and stared at Ander with a worried look that this story had some truth to it, especially the last part. He waited for his companion to laugh in disbelief. When Ander didn't, he continued.

"Ander, she says both guys are floating in the air. When she screamed holy hell, both heads turned to look at her. She says they're spurting blood from their eyes, and both have forked tongues and fangs. Well, Butters might be soft in the sober department but she never misses Sunday Mass at St. Petronilla's. She showed me this little angel thing that she has full of holy water. She threw it at them."

War continued, the muscles in his jaws tensing, "Next thing she knows the door to the trailer slammed open by itself, and the one and one-half, whatever it was, is hurled out the door by an invisible bouncer. Then according to her the door slammed shut."

Ander recognized a hint of fear in War's eyes. He saw the same look in his face that morning when he stared in the mirror. War knew how to recognize a liar; however, Butters convinced him she spoke the truth.

Stroking his chin, Ander regarded his friend. "I take it this guy disappeared by the time you got there?"

"Yeah. I asked Butters about his name, his description, what he vehicle he drove, and she's looking at me as if I'm speaking in Chinese. I'm not sure if she doesn't know, or she's so scared of this guy she doesn't want any reason for him to pay her a visit."

"How about the neighbor?"

"Nadine said she heard yelling and the sound of things breaking, but when she got outside, only Butters stood there."

"That's one hell of a story."

War snorted under his breath. "I can imagine the sergeant's face when he reads my report." He turned back to his pie with the melted ice cream, and wolfed down a few mouthfuls.

"Hey buddy, gotta go I have to be at roll call."

Officer Warrensburg slapped down money to cover his bill and a tip, grabbed his hat and headed out the door.

Ander looked at his untouched sandwich and picked at it; replaying in his mind the story he heard. The fan over his head clacked with the rhythm of a metronome. Mindy stopped by once to ask if he wanted something else, and then left the bill under the saltshaker in front of him.

He paid for the meal, and once outside looked around him as if seeing everything with new eyes. A foreign city, with nothing of the familiar to anchor and comfort him to the ignorance he once lived in.

Obviously, the only place to find answers lay in a visit to the Aquarius Mobile Park. Ander turned on the truck, put on his sunglasses, and the Smith and Wesson Bodyguard 380 clipped against his waist calmed his worries. He looked at the sun trying to estimate how much hours of daylight were left. He then stared down at his lap in a moment of introspection. Ander, no stranger to the horrors of war, had memories floating in his head that would never leave him until he died. He did not suffer from PTSD, or the depression so many veterans experienced, but now he had to admit he feared nightfall.

From inside his mind, but apart a voice whispered, "I am watching over you." How did he forget about Ema?

It didn't take long to arrive at the Aquarius Mobile Park. At the entrance to the road, a large truck stop dominated the intersection. Eighteen-wheelers maneuvered around each other; a neon sign advertised food, fuel and a place to take a shower.

The red pickup drove up a rutted road that led to an entryway. An iron gate off its hinges stood propped against the fence surrounding the park. It could not be mistaken for an upscale, well-maintained, fifty-five and over mobile park. Here, most residents were one paycheck away from homelessness.

Children and animals milled about. A woman watering her miniscule front lawn stared at him with suspicious eyes, as his brand new truck rolled by. It stood out like the proverbial red thumb.

Ander looked at the RVs, some of them sitting precariously on cement blocks. Finding Butters' 1970-era house trailer would be near impossible unless he went door to door. Further, ahead in the middle of the park he saw the mailbox center. A lanky, teenage boy leaned against a pillar, leafing through a magazine.

He signaled over to him, and curiosity sparked in the boy's eyes as he walked over to the truck.

"Hey, do you know where Butters lives?"

"Who's asking?"

"Someone who has a message for her." Ander held a five-dollar bill in his fingers and extended it out to him. "I'm not looking to cause problems for her, just make sure she's okay."

The boy snatched the money from his hand, and pointed towards a narrow avenue. "Take a left when you get down there, she's at the end of the block. You can't miss it, she's got a shitload of gnomes on her lawn."

Ander followed his instructions, and stopped the truck in front of a narrow mobile home with dingy green siding. It sat catty-corner and remote on the edge of the park. A metal awning leaned sideways over the front window. Terracotta planters and gnomes posed on garden stones underneath it. Patches of dry grass poked with desperate fingers among the greedy weeds, which had taken over the space.

Ander walked towards the shallow stairs that led to the front door when a voice halted his steps. "She ain't there."

A skinny woman smoking a cigarette, and sitting on an aluminum lawn chair looked at him with curious eyes. Her crossed feet stuck out of pink flip-flops; the toenails were dirty and grubby-looking.

His voice remained calm, his gaze steady. "Are you Nadine?"

The woman's eyes widened, and the cigarette held in her lips trembled. Her reaction confirmed her identity. She stood up in a slow and measured pace, and Ander suspected she planned to run inside her home.

"Nadine, I'm not looking for trouble. I came to talk to Butters, but if she's not here, please spare me a minute." Ander spoke to her in a soothing tone. He had been a medic in the most stressful scenarios, and he knew how to calm a human being.

The woman pushed her graying blonde hair behind her ear with a nicotine-stained finger. "Sure, I can talk to you a little." Ander smiled, and she returned it, but a hint of caution lurked in her eyes.

"Do you know when Butters will be back?"

A grin overtook her features. "Who knows when that gal will be back? She packed her clothing, took her skinny cat and went to visit her momma." Nadine puffed on her cigarette, shaking her head. "She took so many things; I don't think she'll be back in quite a while."

"Is it because of what happened last night?"

The mirth on Nadine's face evaporated. Her eyes rolled around like a startled horse. "Oh no, no, no, I ain't talking 'bout that! No siree, no." She crossed herself, and kissed a small, silver crucifix hanging around her neck.

Ander took a step closer to her. "Nadine, I know what happened."

He realized by her reaction that she saw more than she told War. "I can tell you're frightened, and I would like to hear about what you saw".

Then she did something unexpected. She busted out crying in large gulping breaths. "Ya damn skippy I'm frightened. I ain't been able to sleep more than half an hour at a time." Large tears welled in her eyes, and she brushed away snot coming from her nose with the back of her hand.

"If I had a place to go, I would've beat Butters out the front gate. I ain't got no momma, nobody that'll let me stay with them."

Ander saw that whatever she saw, scared this woman enough to make her want to leave her home.

"Nadine, the only thing I can tell you is that I'll believe you."

The older woman looked at the stocky man who stood before her. A gash on his forehead marred his handsome face. His hazel eyes were direct and honest, and he exuded masculinity. He wore clean jeans, a leather bomber jacket and sturdy boots, which would have screamed "boring" to a teenage Nadine. Forty years later, she recognized what her grandma called husband material. Reliable men looked like this, and so did bitter regrets.

Fearful images ran riot in her memory. In response she pulled out another cigarette from a little sequined purse, and lit it with shaking hands.

"I've seen some weird shit in my day, and Butters has brought home some real winners, if you know what I mean. Talk about looking for love in the all the wrong places, that was Butters all right."

The thin woman looked all around her, as if fearing someone would overhear her. The trailers were at the edge of the park. A tall chain-link fence with barbed wire demarcated the perimeter; beyond it drying woodland and abandoned cars painted a dreary landscape.

Nadine took a deep drag from the cigarette. "Well, I'm cozy inside my house watching some horror flick. Suddenly I hear this screaming, cussing and the sound of heavy stuff being thrown coming from Butters' place. I've heard this tune before. So I stepped out on my little porch, holding my phone in case things get too out of hand, and then I see…" At this point, she gulped and her eyes flicked at Ander trying to gauge what his reaction would be to her next words.

"I see something, or someone somersault out of her front door. Then her door slams shut by itself. The only light is coming from my porch lamp, and I'm seeing what I think are two guys fighting on the ground, except they're sounding like they're dogs, not humans."

Her face grew strained as she pondered for a moment what effect her next words would have.

"Then it stands up, and it's only one guy! Where'd the other one go? This old guy looks at me, and he's slurping this long, forked tongue back into his mouth. What the fuck! Then he turns around, and clears the fence as if he's walking on air. He parked his truck a bit down from here. Lots of truckers do it when they don't have a trailer attached."

Nadine crossed the narrow road, the pink sweat pants she wore hanging off her bony hips. She went up to a corner where the chain link separated from the metal post. She pushed it, and the opening would allow a person to squeeze through. "You should see some of the foot traffic coming through here on booty call night."

The gossip in her became subdued, when as if on cue a floodlight turned on illuminating the narrow trail on the outside of the fence line. "He climbed in his truck, put it in reverse and drove outta here like the hounds of hell were nipping at his heels".

The floodlight reminded Nadine that nightfall approached closer every minute, and she pulled her purple sweater tighter around her as she walked back to her porch. She climbed the narrow steps and went back into her little sanctuary area.

"Nadine, did you see printing on his truck; a name or a company?"

She hesitated, torn by conflicting emotions. "It was in some cursive writing, and I think it was his name Earl, something or other."

"Earl?" Ander repeated and looked down at his boot, thinking it would take time to run this guy down.

"Jesus, Mary and Joseph!"

Ander's head shot up, and he saw Nadine looking over his shoulder with a horrified look on her face. He turned around, and saw a man standing on the other side of the fence staring at them. His hair gray, greasy and frizzled fell across his eyes. He wore a red, flannel shirt, mussed and full of dry leaves.

"That's him!" She pointed, wriggling her hand up and down, giving off a scared bleat at the sight of the man.

Ema vibrated inside of him. It felt as if all his internal organs and fascia net shifted under his skin. Her voice within, but apart whispered in his mind, "Do not fight what you will see and feel. You will learn the first lesson in being my pocket. This is the price of your life, but do not fear me, because I will never hurt you."

Ander stared off into space and externalized his inner monologue, "Pocket? What's a pocket?" He felt a hard tug in the center of his back that corresponded to the area of his solar plexus, and then his consciousness rocketed backwards. The feeling compared to riding the highest, backwards roller coaster. He found himself an observer inside of his own body. It did not respond to his commands.

Ander's body turned to look at Nadine, and her cigarette fell out of her mouth. "What the fuck!" the woman yelled. She looked into green eyes that did not belong to the man she spoke to only five seconds before. Nadine stumbled backwards, leaving one of her pink flip-flops stuck on the step like a child's forgotten toy. She crawled on all fours to the front entrance, pulled open the screen door and scrambled inside.

Ander turned and shouted. "Hey lady, that's a great story. I'm meeting my editor later tonight at the Lunch Car, and if she gives the thumbs up, the check will be in the mail." He turned around, and the man still stared at him.

He shouted out, "Hey dude, you live in this park? If you got any crazy trailer park stories, I'll pay you for them."

Kyle Earl Kosheen stared at the young man through the chain-link fence. He then looked at the bright, red truck.

Ander then shouted to him again, "Nice ride, huh? So do you got any stories? Hey, you can meet me at the Lunch Car Cafeteria and I'll pay you cash. I'll be there at 9 p.m. tonight." Ander took two steps towards him, and the man walked back into the cover of the trees. Ander followed his progress as he cut across the woods, and then he made out the roar of an engine and the semi's air brakes. The crunch of tires followed it, and then the squeal when they hit the asphalt of the abandoned parking lot that sat next to the desolate patch of forest.

He walked over to Butters' trailer. He pulled out a little statue half-hidden by a shrub. A cement statue of a fairy covered in green lichen smiled impishly at him. His right hand heated up, and then he touched the cool surface of the statue and he said one word, "Salis".

The girlish, frozen face of the figure blinked and then smiled. It shrugged its thin shoulders and flakes of cement flew off it, and the dull gray of the stone faded like if someone dropped a palette of watercolors across it. The fairy fluttered its wings, and they became transparent veined with threads of gold in them.

The little figure curtseyed before Ander and then smiled, as a stone flower it held became a basket. It took flight and came up to his face, and he saw the delicate lavender tint of its skin, and the golden almond eyes as it fluttered before his face like a hummingbird. It dipped its finger into the basket, and then pressed it to his lips. He tasted salt. The lithe fairy then flew off to pour salt at the doorstep of Nadine's trailer. He saw it then flit off along the grass, pouring it along the property line where her trailer sat.

Ander stepped over to a gnome statue bent over in a mooning position, with a mischievous grin on its face. Inside himself, Ander laughed when he saw his hand rub the little, exposed cheeks of its buttocks. The faded colors brightened. It straightened out, pulled up its pants, then removed his pointy hat before bowing like an Elizabethan courtier. Ander pointed at the corner where the fence separated from its post. The little figure kicked it heels, ran over then dived into the post and melted into thin air.

Ander still under Ema's control walked to his pick-up, and maneuvered it out through the narrow streets of the park. He went to the truck stop, where a hive of movement rotated 18-wheelers and regular vehicles around fuel pumps. In the back of the mart, hot dogs rotated on a cooker, next to cellophane wrapped pastries and sandwiches. He prepared coffee as conversation swirled around him.

Standing in line to pay, he looked out surreptitiously through the large glass wall of the building. Ander spied what he hoped for; the man in the red flannel shirt stood next to a group of trucks parked in an adjacent lot. With coffee in hand, he strolled to the red pick-up, feeling the man's unfaltering stare that followed his every move.

Once inside the truck, he saw himself pull out his phone and dial a number he did not recognize. A man with a strange accent answered and Ander said only one word, "Columba". The man replied in a low voice above a whisper, "Please wait one moment". Within seconds, he said, "Yes". Then Ander responded with, "Alexandria, Louisiana". The line went dead, and the call ended.

Ander felt his arms tingle all the way to his fingertips as control of his body returned. He almost jumped out of his shoes when his phone rang unexpectedly. He saw Donny's number light up the display.

"Hey Donny, what's up?"

"Ander you sound good, how are you feeling?"

"Better, though taking it slow."

"I've got a job for you, and before you say no, listen to what it involves." He took Ander's silence as a yes.

"I've got a few gents that want to go out to the gulf for a few days, and have a good time fishing and partying. They want to try their hand at the blue marlin, Mahi and tuna that feed along the blue side of the rip line. I need you to consult on what I should take, in case of any medical emergencies. I'm using a captain and crew I've worked with before, but I would like you to question them, and see if they're up to snuff on what to do if one of these bastards keels over or something."

Ander hesitated, and Donny added, "I'm at the New Orleans office. You can even bring that pretty girlfriend, what's her name, Em? Make it a romantic getaway with her. What do you say?"

Ander listened to Ema whisper "yes" inside of him.

"Ok, Donny, when do you need me down there?"

"Between now and Sunday, I'm hoping to leave on Monday."

"I'll let you know when I'm in town."

Donny asked with deceptive calm, "So are you going to bring Em?"

Ander looked at the phone wondering at the man's sudden interest in his personal affairs. He answered with quiet emphasis, "I don't know."

"All right, see you soon."

Ander searched for the red, flannel shirt among the other figures walking to their trucks, but he had long since disappeared.

XIII. Mind How You Go

TO KILL A FEW HOURS UNTIL 9 PM, Ander went to a Wal-Mart located close to the restaurant. Even though he compared the last forty-eight hours of his life to an acid trip, stocking up with food still demanded his attention.

A tide of people swept him into the store. Ander pushed along a shopping cart, maneuvering around a couple picking out vegetables. To think not too long ago he belonged to this sea of humanity; the ones who were ignorant that werewolves and beautiful women who lived inside of you existed.

He picked out some fresh fruit, two steaks and headed to the dairy section. His steps halted when a high-pitched, feminine voice called out, "Ander. Ander honey, over here."

"Shit." Ander said under his breath.

A woman with short black hair, and dark eyes walked towards him. Gold bangles jangled as she signaled to him, her long, scarlet-tipped fingernails waving in the air. She carried herself with a confident air; aware of the appreciative glances she got from the men who looked at her swaying hips. She poured herself into a pair of floral jeans, and her sandals trimmed in shiny lame fabric winked from the overhead lights.

"Darlin' long time no see. I didn't know you were back in town." She purred, hugging his arm to her breasts.

Ander looked down at Josie Aigrelet, his on and off lover. She owned a successful beauty salon, and when they first met, he stepped into the void left between husbands. Josie embroiled in her divorce proceedings, indicated she wanted a 'no strings attached' relationship, which suited him fine. The affair cooled down when Josie met a new beau, and married him soon thereafter. Only six months later, Ander found a message from Josie waiting for him when he returned from a job. She invited him for dinner, which translated into the death knell for the last marriage.

Earthy and sensual, Josie's sense of humor made him laugh when she would recount stories she gathered from her customers at the salon. He needed a recovery day after spending the weekend at her home.

However, now he sensed a change in her. He felt "Husband No. 4" written on his forehead, and when she looked at him, speculation gleamed in her eyes. Therefore, he retreated from contact with her. Ander's experience with past relationships taught him how to recognize all the signs. Deep introspection showed him that he kept using his parent's marriage, as the comparison that none of his liaisons measured up to. He also understood he did his own sabotaging, by getting involved with women he knew would never fit the bill.

Josie eyed the bruises on his face. "What happened to you?"

"I totaled the truck, but this is as bad as it got for me."

"Darlin', you need a woman to take care of you. How about I come over, and cook you some supper? Tidy up a bit." She batted her eyelashes at him.

Ander pried her hand off his arm. "Josie, I'm heading out to New Orleans on a job, so I don't think it's a good idea."

She pouted, and grabbed his arm again pinioning it between her breasts. "Not even for a little while?" she asked breathlessly.

Ander stepped around her, grabbed a quart of orange juice and said, "No. I gotta go, need to pack some things at home."

He wheeled his cart off before she protested. He wondered why a manager from the vegetable department gave him the stink eye as he rolled by. The balding man with the florid face glared at him with confrontational eyes.

"What the hell is wrong with him?" Ander thought to himself.

He stood at a short line leading to a register for those buying twenty items or less, and when he turned around, he saw the red-faced man arguing in a low voice with Josie. Her mouth set in a stubborn line spoke volumes. She didn't answer vegetable guy, and just folded her arms across her chest. Ander laughed to himself; because he knew Josie just ended that relationship, even though the poor fellow didn't know it yet.

Brisking from the north, the wind held a cold bite. He zipped his jacket and pulled up the collar. Ander sat in his truck for a moment, and then he listened to Ema whisper to him to move towards the deserted end of the parking lot that sat on the edge of a copse of trees.

He turned off the truck, when an overwhelming lethargy overcame his body and mind. His head lolled back on the seat, and he realized he fell asleep when he woke with a start.

Ander felt like he had slept three days. Ema smiled at him, and with practiced fingers braided her hair. She wore jeans and a green sweater that brought out the color of her eyes. Now he understood why she told him to bring the backpack with her things, before he left the house.

"Man if you bottled the way I feel you'd make a mint." he said in a husky voice.

Ema laughed. "Ander this is the easiest way to disengage myself from you. If I do it when you are awake, it will feel like you were kicked in the chest by a mule. It will hurt you, and leave you incapacitated. I will only do it if I have no choice. I do not want to put you at risk, which is why there will be times I hunt alone."

Ander grabbed her hand, "Ema what are we hunting? What are you hunting?"

"Ander I wish there were words I could use to answer your question, but there isn't any because it lies in the experience itself. There are times I am rectifying a wrong or discharging an obligation. Ultimately, I offer redemption."

He questioned her in a troubled voice, "I would have died if you didn't pull me out of the truck, right?"

"Yes, Ander. That is the reason I could be with you the way I am. I cannot be with someone who is meant to keep living. There are times I have joined with a human whose soul flew away, and only the body is left, and I can use it but not the same as with you."

Ander nodded, mulling over her words.

Her voice, deep and dusty said, "Ander I have an important question to ask you. I cannot make you be with me. You have a choice. If you choose not to, I can release you into a painless death. What do you wish to do?"

"Am I your pocket?" he asked soberly.

"Yes, that's what it's called."

His eyes were intent as he stared at hers. In the semi-darkness of the interior of the truck, they glimmered with a luminosity that mesmerized him. "I want to live Ema; I want to be with you."

"Then let's get going to the Lunch Box Cafeteria, and perhaps you'll get an answer as to what we're hunting."

He nodded, straightened up and turned on the truck. A few minutes later, they were rolling into the parking lot of the cafeteria. They sat at a small table. Ander ordered some cheese covered fries and something to drink for both of them. They saw the front parking lot of the restaurant clearly, and no one of interest arrived. They sat there for an hour, and their prey did not take the bait.

Ander looked at his watch. "I think we better leave because you can only pretend to be eating something, and having an interesting conversation for so long."

"I agree, tomorrow we have to go to Alexandria."

Ander stared at her for a minute and then smiled. "You know I feel you work for God's Secret Service, or something."

"You would think of it that way wouldn't you? Well I'm not into martinis, shaken or stirred, my name is not Pussy Galore and I'm not about to call you Mr. Moneypenny."

The streets were empty, as the bright red pickup sped off into the night. Kyle Kosheen sat in a truck he borrowed from a friend, across the street from the restaurant. He wrote the tag number of the vehicle that passed by him. He took his phone, and punched a number into it. A woman's voice answered. She sounded drunk.

There were no niceties in the conversation. "It's Earl. I need payback on the favor I did for you. Remember that meat that went bad on you? Yeah, well I need to know about a tag out of Louisiana, and before you ask, I need to know everything." He gave her the number, and hung up.

The man rubbed a spot between his neck and shoulder. He pulled the shirt away feeling wetness against his skin. Kosheen switched on the interior light of the cabin, and yanked down the visor. In the mirror, he saw the dark red stain of blood. He pulled the shirt, ripping its buttons off. A sharp bite marked the soft area next to his neck. The track of the upper and lower teeth ringed a bloody pool that puckered inwards, like if something bit him from the inside.

XIV. Pocket of Plenty

NADINE DELACROIX SWITCHED ON HER coffeemaker, slipped on her pink flip-flops and with cigarettes in hand stepped out on the porch of her mobile home. Her body felt rested. Sleep came easily, and the sun in her face awakened her that morning. She thought that if she hurried up, she could grab a washing machine in the laundry room before anyone else got there, and then she looked down at her lawn chair. The statue of a gnome wearing a hula skirt stood in it.

She stepped off the bottom step, and stumbled off the narrow path that ran to the street. Arranged in front of her trailer were the gnome statues that used to be in Butters' yard. They held a variety of poses. One shot a bird on both hands, another with sunglasses held a gun and one imitated a biker.

Nadine looked around her, expecting some kids to laugh, because who else would do this. She heard only birds twittering in a nearby tree.

"Stupid kids." she mumbled to herself.

The laundry room echoed in its emptiness when Nadine stuffed her clothes into a machine, and set it to wash. She walked up to the bulletin board to read announcements and ads, when she heard her name being called. The park manager Tina waved a paper and smiled.

"Hey Nadine, guess what? You won this month's raffle."

"I did? What do I get?"

Tina flashed a gift certificate in her face. "It's for a free manicure and pedicure at Just Josie. If you can hold off till next week, I've got an appointment and I'll give you a ride."

Nadine looked at the gift certificate and smiled. Tina told her the date of the appointment, and they agreed to meet.

Later that day Nadine hummed while she took a shower, ignorant of the deep rumble that approached the RV. A police surplus vehicle, badly in need of a new muffler stopped at her door. An unshaven man with dingy clothing stepped from the car. Frederick "Freckles" Pitt needed money. Aunt Nadine, not his real aunt he reminded himself mentally; once married his uncle Royce. Years before the old man got busted for pulling a bank heist. He ended up sentenced to fifteen years in prison, then croaked from cancer five years later.

He'd kept in touch with Nadine because throughout the years he cajoled, or threatened her for a little money here and there. On more than one occasion, he forced her to keep a stash of drugs in her home for a few days. The last time he pulled that one on her she flat out refused him, and he twisted her bony arm hard, leaving a handprint on the skin.

When she sniffled with unshed tears, he told her in a savage voice. "Next time, it'll be your neck I squeeze."

Now he needed to get out of town. He beat the fuck out of his girlfriend, and the neighbors heard the screaming and called the cops. He figured that as bloody as she looked it guaranteed his arrest. When the police arrived, he had fled. Like all simple problems, lack of cash complicated them.

Freckles knew that unless he saw D'Etchepare in the rearview mirror, he would be spending the night in jail.

"Times a wastin'." He said to himself as he pushed away from the car, and walked towards the trailer. Suddenly he lay sprawled out on the ground, staring at the sky. Something stopped his forward impetus, but when he sat up and looked, he saw nothing. Pitt picked himself up, and tried again with the same result. He squatted down to see if a trip wire hid in the tall grass. Then he walked over to Butters' yard, and tried to cross over from that side. This time he knew for sure someone pushed him backwards. His arms flailed around, as he tried to maintain his balance.

Freckles' mind tried to grapple with this conundrum, and all that bubbled to the surface translated to a big fat, "Huh?"

A rock whizzed past his head seconds after he yelled Nadine's name. "What does that old bitch think she's doing?" he thought.

"Fuck Nadine, where are you?" he shouted. Silence answered him, and Pitt felt fury boiling inside of him. He opened his mouth once more, but a rock hit him squarely in the forehead.

"Motherfucker!" he yelled at the top of his lungs. Caught unaware, he stopped because if he didn't know better that gnome statue just moved.

In his befuddled mind, he tried to remember what drugs he took the night before, because he felt his brain had betrayed him.

The neighbor who lived next to Nadine poked his head out, and stared at him hard. He guessed that son of a bitch would call the cops, he could tell.

Freckles got in his car, and turned the clunker towards the exit of the park, fingering the growing bump on his forehead. He stiffened when he saw a police cruiser turning into the narrow road. However, he kept going, hoping to avoid suspicion. Pitt kept his eyes looking forward, as both cars passed each other. Officer Warrensburg decided to check on Butters, and he casually looked at the driver of the vehicle heading towards the exit of the park. Even in profile, he recognized the face of the BOLO flyer they received that morning at roll call.

 He raised dispatch on the radio, and asked for help and a roadblock. War determined that by the time he negotiated the narrow streets of the park, the suspect would have escaped. He remembered two officers were at the truck stop responding to an accident.

Two minutes later, Officer Warrensburg pulled in behind the two police cars that stopped the white vehicle. Freckles Pitt stood handcuffed while an officer patted him down.

The other officer called War over, and showed him the long list of outstanding warrants for the prisoner. The dispatcher's voice crackled over the radio, and informed the officer that several police departments from other jurisdictions would extradite, and go forward with their warrants. War accurately foresaw that Freckles Pitt would go to prison for quite some time.

A week later Nadine got her free manicure and pedicure; she chose two different shades of pink. Tina still sat inside the salon drying her nails, so Nadine wandered down to a small supermarket on the corner of the strip mall. As she stepped in through the doors, she saw an older, black lady trying to pin a notice on a large corkboard. It held business cards, lost dog flyers and notices of different types.

"Honey, you need some help?" she asked the woman.

"Yes baby, I can't stretch my arms up anymore. My arthritis is terrible."

Nadine took an index card and a thumbtack from her. She skimmed the words, and read the job description as an assistant manager at a trailer park.

The old lady touched her arm, and asked her, "Do you need a job?"

Nadine's eyes widened. "Well yeah, but honey I don't have a car. I know this trailer park, Secret Garden, and I have no way of getting there. It's far from where I live off the highway."

The woman studied her through her black, horn-rimmed glasses. Her rheumy eyes searched her face for a moment and then she asked her. "Do you live by yourself?"

"Yes, I do."

"Well this job includes a small trailer on the grounds. I need a person who can go around in the golf cart, and check things out with the tenants. Most of the residents are old folks like me who have a hard time getting around. The park has a locked gate, and every once in a while they forget their code and I need someone to let them in. The pay is not much. Are you interested?"

"Yes, I am." Nadine beamed down at the lady.

"My name is Rosalie, pleased to meet you. So when can you start?"

The two ladies shook hands, and then Nadine's smile evaporated.

"What's wrong?"

"I need to figure out how to get my things over there. I mean, I can start tomorrow, but that's the only hitch."

"That's no problem, just give me your address, and the day after tomorrow my nephews will show up with a truck and bring everything over."

"Really?"

"Honey, they know they have to keep their aunty happy if they want me to bake anymore pecan pies for them."

Two days later two pickup trucks showed up, and loaded all of Nadine's belongings into the back of each. One of Rosalie's nephews pointed to the gnome statues, and asked Nadine if she wanted them. She hesitated a moment and then said yes.

Nadine had already climbed into the truck, when she spied something under her trailer. She ran over, and pulled out a little statue of a fairy. "Where did you come from?" she asked the piece of chiseled cement. She got back in the truck, and carried the figure on her lap.

For the next six months the two dilapidated trailers stood abandoned, but no one could figure out where the riot of wildflowers came from, that grew around and underneath them. The weather turned cooler and drier, but the ground the trailers sat on existed inside an eternal spring.

The gap in the fence stopped being used. Every time someone tried to squeeze through the opening, their gut would wrench and they ran towards the woods, pulling their pants down in order not to soil them.

Several months later, springtime blossomed in eager green everywhere. Nadine stepped out from her trailer, to smoke one of the five cigarettes she allowed herself for the day. Thanks to Rosalie clucking over like a lost chick and feeding her at every opportunity, she put on some weight. She looked at her watch, and saw that landscapers working in the park would arrive in an hour.

Her eyes wandered over the lawn, as she ran through a mental checklist of her tasks for the day. She choked on a puff of smoke, when she saw an extra statue in her small garden. A gnome shooting a moon stood innocently among its companions. She knew the day before it had not been there. All the statues sported a mischievous grin as if they were all in on a big joke.

"I give up." Nadine said to no one in particular.

She stubbed out the half-smoked cigarette, and went inside to trade her pink flip-flops for a pair of pink Converse sneakers. As she tied the shoelaces, she looked at the fairy statue that stood on a table next to her door and said, "You're the only one that understands."

Nadine grabbed her phone and a walkie-talkie, and went outside. She jumped in a small golf cart stationed next to the trailer. She backed it up carefully and as she headed down a garden path, the walkie-talkie crackled. Rosalie's voice reminded her about lunch, and asked if she liked chicken salad.

Butters never returned.

Spring and summer came and went, and the flowers around the deserted trailers disappeared from sight. Both single-wides received a new coat of paint, and still no one wanted to live in them because by then, that corner of the park developed a reputation for being haunted.

XV. This House is Empty Now

THE NEXT DAY EMA GAVE ANDER AN address in Alexandria. They listened to music, content with the little conversation they shared. Their eyes appreciated the landscape that unfolded by them. Before long, they arrived at a stone farmhouse sitting on a few acres of secluded land. A silo and barn peeked over the roofline; they heard the splash of a waterfall from a millpond over the cooing of dozens of pigeons, which looked at them from their cages. Ander followed Ema to a door with the sign 'office' over it. An older woman with a stern-faced expression looked up at them over her half-moon spectacles.

"Name?"

"Columba." Ema replied.

The woman became flustered, "Oh dear, yes, yes we have something for you."

She dropped her pen and picked it up, then it slipped from her fingers once more. All the time she kept stealing glances at Ema.

The woman turned around, and opened one of several small doors that lined the wall behind her. She pulled out a pigeon and handed it to Ema, who removed a paper attached to its leg. She handed the bird back to the woman, as she scanned the message.

The woman asked, "Do you need to send a reply?"

"No." Ema replied flatly and left the office.

Ander followed Ema to the truck. Once there she told him to drive somewhere secluded away from the farm. Ander nodded, and remembered a lookout point under some towering cypress trees they passed on the way there.

Back inside the office, the stern-faced woman went to her desk, pulled out a bottle of whiskey and poured a shot. She tossed it back with relish; her husband walked in and looked at her in disbelief.

"Esther, is something wrong?"

Frowning into the glass, she told her husband, "Columba, picked up a message."

"Is it a man or a woman?" Curiosity tinged his voice.

"A woman, but a man accompanied her."

"What did she look like?"

Esther looked at her husband with troubled eyes. "I can't remember. I think the man had red hair, but I'm not sure."

The farmer stared at the woman in silence for a moment. The cooing of the various pigeons mocked her answer. "What do you mean you can't remember? They were here a few minutes ago."

She looked at her husband. "I mean exactly that. I can't remember, it's like a blur with no details."

He turned to look out the window to the now empty parking lot. "I wonder if it's true."

"If what is true?" his wife asked.

"They say that account has existed for hundreds of years. No one is sure for how long. It's a myth that has existed among those who keep pigeons as messengers, since time immemorial."

Esther turned back to her desk, and poured herself another shot. Her husband's next words stilled her action.

"You must never speak to anyone of this, ever."

"Why?"

"It's rumored that they find those who have dealt in messages for Columba tortured to death."

"Tortured?" gasped Esther. "Why?"

"They are questioned as to what she looks like. They're not believed, when they say they can't remember."

Esther walked to the front door, and locked it. She turned the sign on the window over to where it displayed 'closed'. The woman grabbed the bottle of whiskey, and climbed the stairs to their apartment. Her husband followed her.

XVI. Alice's Crossing

ANDER PARKED THE TRUCK UNDER THE shade of a tree draped with Spanish moss. A mockingbird set up a song from a nearby branch, and a wood thrush answered with its own call.

Ema reached into her backpack, and brought out a simple flip phone. She placed a call, then spoke a series of numbers, and waited. She switched to speakerphone so Ander could overhear the conversation.

A man's voice answered, "You honor us with your call. My grandmother has asked me to beg your indulgence, and meet with her. She is elderly, and it is only the direst need that has caused our family to ask for your help."

Ema asked, "GPS?"

The man paused a moment, and the shuffling of paperwork made crackling noises. Several people asked each other for the information. The man spoke again. He provided the location using the coordinates she asked for.

Ander entered the information into the truck's mapping system. Ema said, "6 p.m. today." and hung up.

Ander looked at Ema and asked, "I take it we're heading there?"

"Yes."

They were riding in silence for over an hour, when Ander looked over at Ema. She stared out the window at the scenery slipping by like a colored ribbon.

"Ema, are you okay? Is this something you can tell me about?"

She turned to him, and smiled, "Ander I haven't been with a pocket like you for about one hundred years. I'm not used to having someone to talk to."

Ander raised his eyebrows at her, and smiled back. "Is that good?"

"This last human I joined with had lost her animus, her soul. Her body kept breathing and functioning as if she were sleeping. No interaction with her, inside or outside of her body occurred. A few days ago, the place we lived at burned to the ground under mysterious circumstances, when I hunted on the far side of town."

His eyes caught, and held hers. "It wasn't accidental?"

"No. Coincidences seldom happen to me, and those around me."

His eyes darkened with a dangerous glint. "Ema what happened with me, this call for help from these people, is this all connected or am I being paranoid?"

Her lips thinned with anger. "I'm not sure how, but I think it is. There is such a thing as Divine Order, but I sense the hand of someone behind the scenes trying to disrupt this order."

Ander looked out the windshield his mind in turmoil. "Who would want to do this?" he asked.

Her brow creased with worry. "Ander when Divine Order is disrupted it will try to right itself again, but this doesn't happen instantaneously. If someone were trying to meddle in the sequence of events, this would be the time to do it. It is much easier to remove a person, than alter anything else that exists in our dimension, in this reality."

Ander listened in bafflement at her next words. "The night of your accident, do you think it coincidental that I traveled on that road?" She shook her head and continued, "A day before, a being visited me in dreamtime, asking for my help. I altered my course because of the message she gave me."

He trembled with intensity. "Who is she?"

"The mate of the creature that attacked you." Ema looked at his face to gauge the effect of her words.

"Tell me everything Ema, I can handle it." Ander stated, looking into her eyes.

"The message I received described how a dark spirit took over her mate. Even his own pack feared him. I don't believe it would have attacked you otherwise. We were destined to meet eventually; perhaps you would have an accident, because of some other cause. The dog man tried to kill you, before we could cross paths."

Ander's eyes swept the road in front of the truck, and then turned back to Ema's face.

Her eyes looked troubled, when she said, "Ander I cannot bring the dead back to life, nor join a human whose body is mutilated."

He remembered all the crazy stories he heard when he served in Afghanistan. Things seen in deserted villages, phantoms that would appear around the outskirts of a military camp, and then vanish in the blink of an eye. Wounded men he attended as a medic, would babble about strange figures trailing their patrol. He chalked it up to the stress of war. Now that he found himself in this unseen world, he realized many of those stories were true.

Ema put her cool hand over his, as it rested on the center console. "You asked me who would want to do this, I believe it's not a who, but a what. Perhaps its disguise is a human pocket, but it's powerful enough to direct other dark spirits to do its bidding. Evil beings are by their nature distrusting, and do not serve another unless it coerces them to do so, especially if it knows it will come up against me."

He shot her a twisted smile. "Are you telling me you're the Dirty Harry of monster world? What would you do to them Ema?" and his smiled broadened.

Ema stared back at him in silence and then smiled. She reminded herself that Ander had yet to experience the full measure of the metaphysical world that surrounded them.

"Ander they fear me because I am the road to redemption, forgiveness and the light. When you are a creature of the darkness, and your nature is deception, acknowledging the error of your ways only results in transformation."

His smile faded a little as he said, "Ema, I am not a coward, but I don't have a problem admitting that I don't understand a lot of what you're telling me. This scares me. I'm just an ordinary guy."

Raising fine, arched eyebrows, she protested, "What is wrong with ordinary? Being average and anonymous are qualities overlooked by the foolish. I am a good judge of character Ander; I have no qualms about hunting with you."

Before he said another word, she stopped him, "I will answer your next question, because I know what it is." She paused, and he looked at her with expectant eyes, "No, I can't read your mind, even when I am inside of you, and you can't read mine."

Ander laughed a little, and rubbed his face a few times. "You sure you can't read minds?" He looked sideways at her, "How did you know I would ask that?"

"Years of practice."

"How many?" he asked, almost afraid of the answer.

"Come grasshopper, when you can snatch this pebble from my hand, you may leave this place." She mimicked the 1970s Kung Fu show about the lessons taught by a Shaolin monk.

Ander laughed, "I get it, enough with the questions."

"So, are you hungry?" he asked changing the subject.

"Yes."

They went through a drive-through and within minutes were back on the road, both of them eating in amiable silence.

The sun traveled westward across the sky, and the red truck followed it. They were a few miles from their destination, when they saw a miniscule historical area off to the side with a marker leaning sideways in the middle of it. Ema told him to stop there.

Before stepping out of the truck, Ema once more used her phone to call a number she punched in. She gave new instructions to the person listening, "The number delivered to

Columba, give them these new coordinates and tell them I am waiting. Only two persons may come." She gave the listener the GPS coordinates of the marker, and hung up.

The small park seemed deserted, and two, lonesome squirrels sat under the branches of the tall pine trees watching them. The shadows were lengthening across the sidewalk that ringed the memorial.

Ander walked around stretching out his legs, at the same time assessing if danger lurked close by. The feel of his gun clipped on his belt comforted him. Ema walked to a marker with a commemorative plaque next to it. Ander ambled over to where she stood reading it.

The small cement obelisk engraved with the words 'Alice's Crossing' stood slightly tilted to the side. The cast bronze plaque read:

For approximately 20 years, a woman known only as Alice operated a trading post at this spot. She lived alone and sold goods to settlers, miners and desperados that were heading westward in search of their fortune. It was rumored that as a child the Comanche stole her only to return her four years later to her people. In 1851, they found her dead among the charred ruins of the cabin she lived in. There was no sign of violence on her body. Indomitable spirits like her opened the gateway to the American West.

Ander read the story, and said absentmindedly, "I wonder what happened to her."

Ema answered in a rush of words, "She died of yellow fever and a young man named Morti set fire to her cabin, and the trading post."

He turned, and gaped at her, "How would you know that?"

"Because, I was Alice."

XVII. Lost Days

A BLUE METALLIC, LATE MODEL MERCEDES SUV slid along a road heading eastbound from Sugar Land, Texas. Gerald Zhu drove the car, disguising the fact that he wished he could make it fly. His grandmother, Ella sat next to him, grim and silent. A few minutes later Gerald looked at the display on the dashboard of the car. He saw less than two miles remained before they reach their destination.

He turned to the old woman, and said in a subdued voice, "Grandmother, are you sure about this? I know you are desperate. We are all desperate. What if this interferes with the police's investigation?"

Ella Zhu turned her head, and looked at her grandson. Her wrinkled face, and eyes betrayed no emotion. She chose her words with care, "I will speak to this woman, and you will stand there and listen. Only listen. If she does not help us, then I fear there is nothing the police or anyone can do."

Gerald saw the turnoff, and he eased the car onto a narrow road that led to a small area surrounded by tall pine trees. He parked next to a red pickup truck. A man and a woman stood by a bronze historical marker. They were both dressed in blue jeans, and light jackets. The man's face appeared bruised; perhaps the result of a fistfight he wondered. He didn't know what he expected, but he realized in that moment he hoped it amounted to more than this. They looked so ordinary. He turned the car off and stared at them.

Ella Zhu grabbed the handle of the door, and tried to exit the vehicle. "Grandmother, stop!" he said to her as he lunged from his side of the car, and ran around to where she stood on unsteady legs.

He held out his hand, and helped her to walk. Her gray hair pinned to the top of her head framed a wrinkled, but kind face. Expensive, loose-fitting clothes floated around her as she hobbled towards where Ema and Ander stood.

When she reached them, Ella let go of her grandson's hand, and doddered forward. She saw a woman with deep red hair, and grayish-green eyes. Her skin appeared translucent and unwrinkled, and she guessed her age could not be over thirty-five. She fit the description of the woman who took her grandmother from Laramie to Santa Fe in 1879.

She turned to her grandson, and in a curt voice said, "Bring here what I asked for."

Gerald sprinted back to the car. He came back with two cushioned, collapsible chairs.

Ella turned to Ema, "Please sit. I am afraid my legs will not permit me to stand."

Ema sat, still not uttering a word, and Ander bent over and whispered in her ear if he should stay. She just nodded.

Ella realized that despite her age, little in her life prepared her for this conversation. Born the youngest of five children, she had been spoiled and petted as the only girl. Her grandmother claimed her as the favorite of her grandchildren. There were so many wonderful stories the family matriarch told her, and she sat entranced at her feet not caring if they were true or not.

Gerald stood behind his grandmother and squeezed her shoulder in reassurance. She affectionately patted his hand. The old woman took a deep breath and said, "My name is Ella Zhu, my grandmother was Jin Wei."

Ema's tone remained cool and impersonal. "That is the only reason I am here. I am in her debt."

Ella recognized in those few seconds, there were many secrets her grandmother never disclosed to anyone. "My family did not know of this debt. My grandmother told me if ever a dire need for help arose, which money, intelligence or power could not resolve that I should send for you. Good fortune has smiled on my family until now. Until three days ago."

Ema's voice remained carefully colored in neutral shades. "Do not speak to me of suspicions or theories; tell me exactly what has happened."

Despair and helplessness swept through the old woman. She looked at Ema with the eyes of a drowning person, knowing this woman held salvation for her family in her hands. "Someone stole my great granddaughter away. They kidnapped her."

Ema kept studying the woman's face in silence.

The old woman continued, "We have notified the police, but I know that they cannot find her because a demon stole her."

Ema stood up, and held up her hand to stop the old woman from speaking further. Behind her Ander put his hand over his gun. He looked around, but saw no one except the four of them.

Ema clapped her hand once, and said, "Os rouge."

Nothing happened, and Gerald groaned inside of himself, thinking as far as theatrics were concerned, the word cheap came to mind. Only his grandmother's insistence had convinced him to attend this meeting, and now here he stood feeling like a damned idiot.

Surprised when he felt the temperature drop; his skin prickled in response to the cool air that settled over them. A melancholy wind whipped the pines into a mournful sighing. It affected no other tree outside the perimeter of the little memorial area. Dark clouds scudded across the sky blocking out the setting sun.

Even without an overhead sun, shadows melted away and congregated under the trees, where several figures shifted and moved. Campfires flickered in the darkness there. Men squatted around the dancing flames that sprung from orange pulsing, embers. They wore old-fashioned clothing. Suspenders held pants in place, and well-worn hats sat back on their heads. Revolvers hung from most of their waists. Further along, several Comanche warriors sat on their ponies and stared impassively at the group.

Ander observed the Asian man across from him take a deep breath, and clutch the back of the chair where the old woman sat. Ander thought to himself, "This is pretty tame, so far."

Ella saw the figures, and glanced away, afraid to let her eyes linger too long in their direction.

Ema sat down once again. She told the group, but to no one in particular, "Even the dead serve a purpose and they are in my debt, I am giving them a chance to discharge it, and I am protecting them as well."

Ema looked at Ella, and asked her, "Why do you think a demon took your great-granddaughter?"

Ella cleared her throat, and said, "Jin Wei told me the story of how the man that sold her to Grandmother Gussie wanted her back, because they promised her to a demon. He said that since her real mother died, the demon demanded that the child she carried in her belly be substituted in her place. It would not be denied its tribute, even though many years passed. I think Grandmother Gussie guessed the man, driven by desperation might try to steal her. That's when she asked you to bring her to Santa Fe."

Ella paused a moment, thinking what her next words would be. "Jin Wei always told me that this demon would not forget what they owed it, and that eventually it would come to claim its prize."

Ema inhaled through her nose, and closed her eyes for a moment. The tremor of evil whipped around the edges of the barrier she summoned. She recognized the spirits that waited for Alice's return were also at risk. If there were no truth in what Ella said, nothing from the dark world would have been drawn to their meeting.

Ella continued, "Of all the stories my grandmother told me, she insisted I remember this one especially towards the end of her life. She made me promise I would pass it on to another family member before I died."

"Ella, why do you think it has chosen this person?"

The elderly woman wiped away a tear from the corner of her eye. "She is the last child born into our family. She is intelligent, innocent and unaware of the power of her beauty. Her name is Jenny, the name given to Jin Wei by Grandmother Gussie. In the days before she disappeared, she suffered from horrible nightmares, and her screams would awaken the entire household. She kept saying that something watched her from the corner of the room. I told Jenny the story for the first time, two weeks before she disappeared, and I thought the nightmares were because of this. How could I have been so wrong?"

A sob broke from the woman's lips. "The police say that she might have run away because they found her car abandoned. They found no sign of a struggle or blood. She is nineteen years old, and as an adult, they told us she is free to leave. There have been no demands for ransom. The police do not understand that she would never do this."

Ema looked up to Gerald, "Where did they find her car?"

He straightened up, and pulled a card from his wallet and a small pen with a built-in flashlight. He jotted the information on the back, and handed it to Ema.

"They found her car with no mechanical problems parked on the shoulder of the road. The place is remote. It's a trucking lane, and the only thing we can come up with, is that we have a warehouse for the business not too far from there."

As an afterthought, he added, "Our family will give anything to have Jenny returned to us. If they want money, we will agree to their demands."

Ema slipped the card into the pocket of her jeans. "It doesn't want money Gerald."

He looked at Ema, and it took him a moment to realize she called him by his given name, without being told that information beforehand.

Ella took a hold of Ema's hand, and said, "There is a longing in my heart, it feels as if this yearning will remain unfulfilled. I fear this hole in my soul will never heal if Jenny does not come back to us. Jin Wei always told me you were kind, and that she never forgot those days spent on the desert traveling to Santa Fe."

Ema held the old woman's frail hand. "She nursed someone that I cared for on that trip. Her hands were always kind. That is the debt I owe her."

"The tall man, with hair like a lion's mane?" Ella asked her.

"Yes." Ema answered.

Darkness engulfed the park, since no light posts had been erected there. The flickering of the campfires under the trees became more noticeable.

Ander stepped back, and kept a watchful eye all around the small group. The bunch of cowboys sitting in the gloominess didn't pose a threat. They just murmured among themselves, and every once in a while he would hear a short laugh float in the air.

The pines still soughed, and once when the wind picked up Ander looked to their tops, and did a double take. Passing back and forth above them, were two or three forms that looked like small dragons with outstretched, bat-like wings.

His attention returned to Gerald, when he asked Ema, "What now?"

She responded with quiet firmness. "You will tell no other person about this conversation, even your own family members. This is for their protection. You cannot tell police, let them continue with their investigation."

"Why protection?" Gerald asked alarmed.

"Ignorance will be their safeguard, but I can't say the same for both of you."

Ella stated, "I do not care about myself, but nothing can happen to Gerald."

Gerald more of a pragmatist asked Ema, "Should I hire bodyguards, what type of security do I need to set in place?"

Ema sensed his disquiet, but she anticipated her next words would not be what he expected. "They cannot offer you the defense you need. Only she can."

Ema pointed to a figure that detached from the plum-colored darkness underneath the pines. It walked towards them, and then stopped. The figure glowed with its own golden luminescence, and the colors of her skin, and dress faded like an old sepia photograph.

"Grandmother!" Ella exclaimed. She stood marveling at what her eyes beheld. The figure did not resemble the old lady of her childhood, instead a young woman wearing a dark, corseted gown stood there. The dress' hem swept the ground, and with a high collar and long, puffed sleeves, she seemed to have stepped from a Victorian-era movie. The figure's lustrous black hair sat in a bun at the back of her neck.

Gerald stared at the figure in silence. He once saw a photograph of this woman, but she wore traditional Chinese garb, and had long since lost her youth. This girl had soft cheeks, and he saw beauty in the curve of her face. To think she created a thriving business in a frontier town with his grandfather, who married her after losing his first family in a sea crossing from China. The figure then disintegrated, the golden lights flying off into the flow of the wind.

Ella faced Ema, her eyes filled with tears. Before they asked the questions, she saw in their faces Ema spoke in a quiet tone, "You are all a part of her. Your blood, your flesh sprung from her womb. Now that we have summoned her, there is no protector more powerful than she is. Go home and wait."

Ella nodded. Gerald folded and gathered the chairs. Ander, who stood behind Ema asked, "What about them?" and pointed upwards.

All eyes followed his finger. Ella gasped, and Gerald dropped the chairs he held.

Ella twirled her forefinger, and a small golden cone of sparkling lights grew upwards until it spun over their heads. It took the shape of an eagle that spread out its wings that spanned at least seven feet in diameter. It flapped them once rising into the air, and the creatures circling over the top of the pines dispersed. The eagle then tucked it wings close to its body, and dove towards the group. It grew smaller until it became the size of a cube, which melted into Ema's outstretched palm.

Ander, Ella and Gerald stared at Ema's hand waiting for something else to pop out. Then all three turned to look at the figures that still waited under the cobalt shadowiness of the pine trees. Golden campfires that issued no heat or made noise, created dancing shadows on their watching faces.

Ema's mouth twitched with amusement. She turned to Ella and Gerald. "It's safe to leave now."

Neither Ella nor her grandson said another word. They left, and once inside the vehicle, Gerald turned towards the old woman and said, "Forgive me grandmother for not believing you."

Ander and Ema's eyes followed the blue vehicle as it turned onto the road, and sped away. He turned to her, and motioned to the figures that milled about underneath the pines, "Are they here because of when you were Alice?"

"In a manner of speaking."

Ander's eyes studied her with a curious intensity. "How long were you out here?"

"Twenty-two years."

"What are they waiting for?"

Ema turned to Ander, and looked directly into his eyes. "These were people invaded by the darkest of entities and demons. No law existed in this land during those years, and they committed atrocities with no fear of repercussion. What you are looking at now are just humans, imperfect and products of those times, but nothing worse."

Ander nodded towards the three Comanche who still waited mounted on their horses.

"One of these abducted Alice as a child. He did not treat her well at all, and egged on the woman that drowned her, which is when I stepped in. The other two like him, welcomed dark creatures that invaded their souls. Their medicine woman told them many times to stay away from Alice, and her trading post. They did not heed her warning. One day they never returned to their camp."

All the figures by the fires stood up, and looked at Ema with unblinking eyes. Ander saw for the first time that there were two women among the figures.

The pines stilled, and the winds that weaved between them dispersed. The twin scents of honeysuckle and gardenia wafted in.

A blue light glowed from the obelisk, and stretched to grow into an arched doorway. Out of the opening walked a little boy. He looked to be five or six years old. Dressed in old-fashioned clothing, he skipped towards the figures in happy abandon. He went up to a grizzled man, with a deep scar that ran across his cheek. The boy took the man's hand, which followed him like a lamb. Once side by side, Ander saw they were the same person.

A procession of children came out of the doorway to claim the adult they became. The pair of them would walk into the blue light, and pass from sight.

The Comanche warriors each pulled up the child they once were, to ride their horses into the luminosity that welcomed them. A little girl with braided pigtails pulled a woman along towards the shining doorway. They stepped in, and disappeared. Suddenly, the child popped out, and blew Ema a kiss.

The blue glow turned into a turquoise shimmer. The arch grew misty and melted into nothingness, and the sweet scent of flowers receded.

XVIII. House of Love

ANDER'S PROFILE, DARK AGAINST THE moonlight turned to Ema. The normal sounds of night filled the small park.

"Where to?" he asked her.

"Let's go get something to eat."

A few minutes' drive from the park, they came to a small restaurant the served Mexican food. Ander looked at the other patrons in the eatery, enjoying their burritos and tacos, unaware that lizard-looking things with wings existed, which made Bigfoot look tame.

He felt a part of him come back from the accident. He experienced an adrenaline rush when he stood at the park ready to defend Ema. No fear; no pain throbbed in his body, only a determination to take on whatever stepped out of the darkness. Not that she needed protecting, so far she played the part of bodyguard to perfection.

Ema stared into the darkness outside the restaurant window. She sat in silence during the meal, and Ander studied her profile, realizing how lonely her existence must be.

She turned back to him, and said, "Let's go to the place where they took her."

A few minutes later, the truck headed into the night. The traffic thinned out as they traveled to the outskirts of the small town. The road became a solitary, two-lane highway.

Illuminated signs that led into small corporate parks, were the only pockets of light. Ema looked at the card, and read the warehouse address for the business Zhu Distributing printed on the front. She showed it to Ander, and a mile further on they found the entrance to the park. A winding road led to a building lined with warehouse doors. The place appeared deserted, and sodium vapor lamps stood like friendless sentinels in an empty parking lot.

Ander lowered the window of the truck, and listened to the sound of insects and night animals that drifted over from the sparsely wooded area surrounding the park. He looked closely at the building, and did not see any lights coming from any office window. The roll-up doors were all down and closed. The truck idled, and then Ander held up his hand. He reversed the truck, and parked it in the dimness cast by a large cement wall where dumpsters, like metal elephants lined up. He turned the truck off.

Ander's expression became taut, "Ema, there's voices coming from the far side of the building."

"What do you think we should do?" she asked him.

"Go around to the other side of this building, and see who's there. It might just be a business open late at night, and this cloak and dagger approach is a little over the top. If not, we'll be glad we're on stealth mode."

Ema nodded. She knew already, no greedy businessman toiled late into the night. The funk of corruption filled her nostrils from the moment they turned off the main road. Unless an abattoir operated out of one of the warehouses, a being that crawled from the bowels of hell walked among the humans there.

They exited the truck, and closed the doors making no noise. Ander studied the area before stepping out of the semi-darkness into the lighted parking lot.

They crossed the asphalted, yellow-lined square, and paused when they were in the gloom cast by the shadow of the building. They walked towards the other end of the wall, creeping forward until they overheard voices.

Ander peered around the edge, and saw a large panel truck backed up to an office entrance. A graphic of falling rose petals with the words 'House of Love Flowers' decorated the side of it. The tag line below it read, 'For Those Who Insist on the Best'. He heard another truck idling, blocked from view by this one. Ander stepped back behind the wall.

Quick steps were approaching were they stood. Ander silently mouthed an invective realizing they had nowhere to hide. Whoever approached them stopped shy of where they hid, and a woman's raspy voice, filled with fury berated a second individual who stayed silent. "I don't know what the fuck is wrong with you, but I contacted you about this transport because the word is that you're reliable, and you keep your mouth shut, but looking at you I have my doubts. If it wasn't because there's a deadline involved, I'd find someone else."

The other person shuffled their feet. A man's hoarse whisper responded, "Look Fanny, I'm just coming down with some bug and I may look shitty, but here I am. I don't beg out from jobs, and leave my clients hanging. So whadya got?"

The woman's voice hardened, "This package is going non-stop to Louisiana. This flower is unique. She better arrive in the same condition she's leaving in." A pause stretched out, "Don't roll your eyes at me fucker, I mean it. The buyer has made a special order for this flower, and if there's anything wrong with the merchandise, you will deal with him, and I guarantee there's no rock to hide under from this guy."

The man's gruff voice changed a bit, and sounded almost hissy, "I don't mix business with pleasure, so shut up. I'm here for the money, just like you. I've been doing these runs longer than you, you two-bit whore, so either give me the merchandise with the instructions and destination, or I'm getting the fuck outta here."

They heard someone clicking on a lighter, and then the burnt smell of cigarette drifted towards them.

Fanny replied tersely, "This flower has been here for three days, and she's being prepared for transport. Just put it in the truck's cab. If it's not delivered at the expected hour, don't even bother to call me, because I don't talk to dead men."

"Yeah, yeah, yeah stop your yapping and give me some of the money you owe me." The man walked away, his steps crunching on the asphalt. The woman kept standing in the same place.

Fanny Foster, one time successful pharmacist looked at the retreating figure of the bedraggled man. Her fall from grace, after running a pill mill with a doctor could only be described as hard and swift. She served some prison time, and after being released, a man approached her about opening a business that would serve as a front. Her business partner, an obscure, but obscenely rich individual who traded in flesh, always remained in the background. She handled the daily running of the business, and she'd met many shady characters. Plenty of crazy ones too, but this trucker scared her.

She pulled her phone from her pocket, and called the manager of a bondage club out of Dallas who recommended him.

"Hey Lydia," she said in a rough voice, "who's this wacko you sent over for my delivery to New Orleans? You know the guy who ordered this flower is a picky son of a bitch; you've dealt with him yourself. He doesn't want to hear excuses about mistakes."

"What?" Fanny responded after a pause, "He asked for this guy by name? Are you fucking kidding me?" She inhaled sharply after a short silence, "He's been delivering packages to him for how long? Thirty years!" The conversation ended.

Fanny stood there a moment. Deep misgivings flooded her brain about this fellow, but then she remembered there were other people coming in for deliveries to other parts of the country. She made a firm commitment to herself though, never to be alone with this lunatic again.

Ander and Ema heard her walk away. They looked at each with a knowing glance; guessing these were the people that took Jenny.

Then they made out the growl of a truck engine revving, and then pulling forward. Ander peered around the corner of the building again. The vehicle on the other side of the panel truck became visible now. A mud-splattered semi, with Earl-E Trucking on the door fit Nadine's description.

Ander pulled back, and thought about what Ema told him about Divine Order. He looked across at Ema and whispered. "I think this is the same truck that Nadine saw at the park."

In answer, Ema stepped around him, and peered cautiously towards the truck. She saw two men carry a long bundle between them. The side door of the cab stood open, and one jumped inside and helped to accommodate it inside. They handed an envelope to a man who stood looking at them. He wore a baseball cap over his greasy, frizzy hair, and his clothing hung on him like a scarecrow. He looked sick, as if his body had lost weight in a short amount of time.

She saw mounted on the roof of the truck what the humans milling about failed to see; the form of a savage dog-like creature. No fur, only scaly skin clung to it bones and ribcage.

Ema motioned for Ander to return the way they came. They were about to step out into the parking lot, when they saw headlights coming from the road that lead into the park. A late model, white cargo van made its way across the space. They eyed it impatiently until it turned the corner of the building, no doubt heading to where Fanny waited for them.

Once inside the truck, Ander looked at Ema, "If that's the guy at the mobile park, he'll recognize me and this pickup."

"That's him, and that delivery is Jenny."

Ander's voice became concerned. "Ema, these are human traffickers. We have to leave this area before we get spotted."

The red pick-up made its way across the parking lot, with its headlights off. Ander held his breath going out the entrance road hoping not to encounter anyone. He tooled the truck forward, and turned eastward on the main highway, guessing it would be the route used by the trucker.

Ema pulled her flip phone from the backpack. She called a number, and read the address of the warehouses from Gerald's card. Her instructions were to notify the FBI, but warned to surveil the scene for the next four hours. If a vehicle left the location, they should ask the local police department to stop it under the pretense of a traffic stop.

The rich timbre of Ander's voice filled the silence, "Ema why don't you have law enforcement pull this guy over?"

Her expression became taut with strain, "Ander whatever is inside that man will kill Jenny at the first sign of a blue light, and then kill himself. A few days ago he wouldn't have, but what's walking with him now will never allow him to be questioned by the police."

"I'd thought of that, but what can we do? Even if we let him pass us by, and trail him on I-10 into New Orleans, chances are we'll lose him."

"There's a rest stop about fifty miles from the state line. We'll wait for him there."

Ander looked at her, "How do you know he'll stop there?"

"I'll make him stop."

"I know you could, but your newbie pocket cannot help being curious how you'll do that."

Ema smiled at him, and he couldn't tear his eyes away from her face. "Have you heard of gremlins?" Ander nodded. "I'm sure you haven't heard of their mean cousins," she added.

XVIV. Duende Fue

THEY PARKED THE TRUCK ON THE FAR SIDE of the rest area, hidden from view by the main building. The old stop had few amenities except for bathrooms, and one machine that dispensed soda, water and small bags of potato chips. The turgid heat of the day swirled under the opaque light that flickered in the main area between the bathrooms. Gang graffiti decorated an empty telephone housing that stood next to a water fountain.

Ander walked back to the truck after using the restroom. He slid into his seat and looked at Ema, the blue light from the dashboard highlighted points on her face. Then he recognized the unmistakable sound of something scrabbling on the leather seat behind him. Within seconds, he stood outside the truck, its door wide open. He looked at the woman who sat with calm ease in the passenger seat. She crooked her finger indicating he should come back into the truck.

Ema smiled as she said, "You didn't give me a chance to warn you."

He rewarded her with a larger smile of his own. "I think you wanted to see how fast I exited the truck."

"Maybe," she admitted, "but I don't want you to panic, because you will feel something touching your head. Just be still."

The smile fled his face, and his eyes grew wide. Skinny, childlike fingers tickled the back of his neck, and threaded his hair. In his mind he questioned, "How bad could something be that likes to stroke my hair?"

Then what sounded like angry hornets grew into words that were unintelligible. A creature that looked like a thin monkey, but with a human baby's face crawled into Ema's lap. The eyes unlike a child's were small, squinty and greedy looking; the nose only two slits and teeth like white needles escaped through the front of its mouth. Its skinny arms ended in three, elongated fingers. Reddish, translucent skin covered the entire body, and its bodily functions quivered and pulsed beneath the surface.

Ander stared at the thing trying to cuddle against Ema, and he swiveled his eyes around realizing that something else still touched his hair. "How many were there?" he thought.

Ema reached out and touched Ander's hand that rested on his knee. Liquid warmth rushed up his arm, and dissolved into his body. The incomprehensible sibilance that poured into his ears became words. The grotesquerie behind him crawled over his shoulder, and joined its companion. One took Ema's hand and stroked it, looking at her with what passed for a smile on these creatures.

"Sweet Sibyllina bid us. Do you need a child's breath stolen, a step made slick with moss, the slip of a knife against flesh?" The creatures looked at one another, and grinned in eager anticipation.

Ema ignored their question, and looked at Ander. "These are known as Duende Fue. Once they were household spirits, or dwelt in the forest; mischievous, sometimes helpful but never bent on spilling blood. Evil however is always intent on seduction of all beings, not just humans. These two have dwelt in the hinterlands between what they once were, and what is consuming the good that is still left in them. They are no longer Duendes, and are forbidden entry to be amongst them, something I suspect they desperately desire."

Ema looked down at the upturned faces of the Duende Fue, "Is that not so?"

Both of them spit like angry kittens. One grumbled, "All I want is to lead a traveler into a pit of quicksand, and watch them for hours while they get sucked down."

The other one piped in, "Or play among vegetables used in a restaurant, setting them to rot early and making all who eat the food sick, and even die!" it ended triumphantly.

Without looking down at them Ema responded in a quiet voice, "Then I have no use for you, be gone."

Both of the creatures nuzzled into Ema's midsection. "Forgive us Sibyllina, gave us a task but not something that is good, perhaps a little bad."

"This is your errand; there is one approaching in a truck. Make it that he has no choice but to stop here. Do not allow the machinery to run again until I tell you."

One of the Duende Fue, looked at Ander like a jealous child. "What about him? Should he fall down, and break his nose? It will go well with the rest of his face"

Ema's tone became icy. "Never harm him. You are to guard him." her voice dropped an octave and sounded like crushed metal, "Do you want to learn what it means when you disobey one such as me?"

The Duende Fue scampered over to Ander's lap. "Forgive merciful Sibyl, forgive."

Ema glowered at them, and then from her fingertip she threw a golden pellet into each one of their mouths, which they opened like small birds. The creatures stood on the wide center console of the truck, and spread out red, veiny wings.

Ema touched the button that slid back the sunroof, and they flew off into the night.

XX. Hunter and Killer of Men

ANDER'S EXPRESSION BECAME incredulous. he looked out through the sunroof's opening. Ema hit the button, and it closed. She left the truck, and stood in the deserted parking lot. Ander joined her. The sound of traffic on the highway drifted over to where they stood.

Her voice cut the silence, "Ander when I draw that man away from the truck, check on Jenny, but do not speak to her, or identify yourself."

"What about when he pulls in, and sees the truck? I'm astounded no one else has stopped in here all this time," Ander said looking around the short stubby lawn crisscrossed by cracked sidewalks. A lone table and bench sat under a tin roofed gazebo.

"When anyone looks at the sign for this rest area, they see that it's closed for repairs."

"Won't this guy keep going?"

"The glamour will dwindle for a moment, but only for him."

Ander stuck his hands in his jean's pockets and rocked back on his heels, studying the woman that stood in front of him. "What about you Ema? Are you going to be all alone, with whatever that thing is driving the truck?" He asked.

"Yes, I am," she said in a soft tone, touched by his concern for her, "but there is more to this situation than a man who

177

kills people, and occasionally provides delivery services for a human trafficking ring."

Then Ema's face became aloof. "Ander, I do not want you to approach me, whatever you see or hear. Instead of helping me you will make me vulnerable."

His gaze held steady, as he nodded. "I get it."

In a matter-of-fact tone, she added. "Look for a pair of handcuffs in the truck, I guarantee you that monster has more than one stashed there."

"Handcuffs?"

"Yes, and he'll be here in a few minutes."

Ander thought to himself, "We will find out if it's true or not that you can read my mind, because if you think I will not help you if I see you're in trouble, you're in for a rude awakening. That son of a bitch is made of flesh and bone, and a bullet in his head will save the taxpayers a lot of money."

He saw that she walked off, and sat at the picnic table. Her backpack lay next to her. They both turned to look at the shine of headlights as the truck came up the exit ramp that led into the rest area. It made a clanging noise as if something had become loose. As Ema expected he drove the truck behind the building, where it could be concealed from view from the main road. The truck belched black smoke from its exhaust pipes, and turned off.

The thin man with disheveled hair jumped from the truck, yelling down the vilest curses ever brought against an inanimate object. He walked around it, climbed inside and tried to turn it on. The engine did not even turn over. He shouted his frustration again. He sat with his feet propped on the step up, and put his head in his hands.

He straightened up, and snarled over his shoulder, "Shut the fuck up! Stop the fuckin' crying! If I hear one more thing out of you, I will pull your teeth out with a plier, and that way you'll give better head."

Kyle Kosheen couldn't think straight. He always kept his truck well maintained to avoid the situation he found himself in, so he couldn't understand why this piece of shit broke down. A month before a mechanic had checked the truck, and assured him it ran like a top.

His head pounded, and his ribcage ached as if it would split in two. He tried to form a coherent thought as to how he would get his truck running, without being arrested. An idea like a worm snuck into his bloated brain. Kill the bitch, dump her body in the woods and get a tow truck out here. The guy expecting this delivery would not be happy either way, so why should he be fucked in the process as well. He'd placate the son of a bitch later; deliver some extra young and tender meat free of charge.

He tried again to get the semi cranked up, but it didn't make a sound. He looked around, and nodded as if in answer to a conversation only he heard. A remote place like this one would be ideal if he decided to dump her body in the woods behind it. Chances are it would never be found.

He saw movement out of the corner of his eye, and turned to see a young girl standing in the dim light of the bulb over the picnic table.

In a timid voice she said, "Sir. Sir, please would you give me a ride?"

Earl stepped down, and ambled closer to the girl. He licked his dry lips and looked her up and down. She wore cutoff shorts, a red tank top and scuffed-up ankle boots. She shivered in the cool breeze, and he saw goose pimples on her arms. A headband of bright red roses nestled in her short, black hair; its color matched the thick eyeliner she wore. Her lips were painted purple so deep they looked black. Cheap tattoos on her arms, and her upper thigh decorated her body.

Like a magnet to steel, he found he couldn't tear his eyes away from her.

"Well honey, what's a bitty little girl like you doing out here by yourself?" he said in his best sugary tone.

Her smile trembled as she said, "Well I got into a fight with my boyfriend, and he drove off and left. I've tried calling him, and he doesn't answer the phone. I guess he's madder than I thought."

"Where you goin' to?"

"Over two exits." She pointed westward, in the opposite direction he traveled in.

"Well, you know for a trucker to lose time he's losing money, but maybe we could come to some arrangement."

He licked his lips, but this time the long tongue that slipped out ended in a slit. His eyes followed her hands as she reached up, and took off her headband. He felt mesmerized by their bright red color. It reminded him of blood. An undeniable thirst came up from the depth of his gut. He savored the metallic scent of blood, as if he tracked a wounded prey.

The girl brought the flowers to her chest and crushed them; their scent like an invisible wave from an endless ocean, enveloped the area.

"I hoped you would say that," said an unrecognizable voice emanating from the girl.

A growl grew in Kosheen's head urging him to run away; warning him to sprint across the highway, and get away from the naked woman that stood in the spot where the girl had been a moment before. The odor of fresh blood anchored him to the spot like a man drugged.

Her burgundy hair waved in a slow rhythm around her, as if she stood inside an invisible sea. One rose melted into her skin. It became a thin cloth that wound around her hips, and then curved upwards over her buttocks. It continued to drape down over each shoulder to cover her breasts. The red silk tied itself over her pubic bone.

The other rose rotated in her hand, and enlarged to become a pink bronze shield that shone like a mirror. From the depths of its infinite reflection, a small snake-like object crawled out and slithered up her arm, around her neck and down her other arm. Once there it elongated and become a long whip, which she cracked once and the air sizzled.

Kosheen fell forward on his knees. He tore his jacket, and then his shirt off. His emaciated torso roiled with a movement from something that wanted to punch a way out of his body.

Ema struck the polished shield with the handle of the whip, and a humming that turned into a dulcet peal sounded around them. Blood burst from both of Kosheen's ears. He cupped them with his hands, and howled in pain.

A face imprinted itself against the skin of Kosheen's belly. It traveled up through the inside of his body. Out of a gash between his neck and shoulder, a black, forked tongue slipped out and lapped at the blood spilling from his ear.

Kosheen opened his mouth, and rotted blood gurgled out and spilled over his chest. A deep, scratchy voice implored, "Free me great Sibyl."

"Name yourself." she commanded.

"You know my name." it responded.

"Then remain unnamed. It will soon be your master, and slaves have no name," the woman said with an air of finality.

It growled in frustration, and deep hatred. "I am known as Scepter."

"Show yourself to me." Ema commanded.

Kosheen writhed on the ground, and the snout of a dog emerged from his back followed by the head, then a pair of human hands grabbed it trying to drag it back inside the body. The man contorted, and with a sucking sound a large dog dripping yellow puss emerged, accompanied by the pollution of rotting flesh. The skin sewed itself back together from the wound left by the demon's exit.

Kosheen curled into a fetal position. Even though his mouth remained closed, moaning came from the prostrate body.

The demon Scepter lay down before Ema. It whimpered, trying to imitate a real canine.

"Do you think," she asked, "that I have time to waste with your deceptions?" In a fluid movement, Ema raised her arm, and the whip arced through the air, and tore a slit in the darkness of the night. A light appeared of such brilliant intensity that only a thousand suns could produce it. Flickers of light, like tiny fireflies emerged and swirled around the opening.

The demon raised itself on its four legs and trembled, stepping back from the light. "Ask what you want of me Wise Woman, I am yours to command," the dog snarled.

"I need not command one such as you. You however have no choice but to obey me. What is inside this man?"

"A vampire." It spat out the words.

"A vampire that competes with you for the body of a man?"

"Its creator is a powerful master, but it has never been a human, it has never owned a human. It does not know how to be stealthy and cunning; and it is obedient only to its thirst for blood. It forced itself into this form, and I will abide no other to be there with me."

"How does one oust an enemy superior to you?" asked Ema in a calm voice, "Do you have your answer yet?"

The gray-skinned dog drew back lips from its black teeth. It growled deep in its throat. Finally, it spoke again, "It seeks the help of one more powerful than all."

Ema looked around her mockingly. "Who has come to your aid?"

The demon lay back down, uttering guttural cries. It submitted to her will.

"Where is he taking the woman in the truck?"

"To a place he has visited many times, always with live flesh. His mind is scattered, and he uses the map in the machine to guide him."

"Why her?"

"She is fulfilling an agreement."

"By who?"

"Many years ago, her forbears promised a proud and fierce demon human flesh in exchange for safe travel across the seas. They never gave the tribute as agreed."

Ema stared at the creature, and narrowed her eyes, suspecting that something else remained undisclosed. "Why is she being taken to New Orleans?"

The dark dog looked up at the woman with red glowing eyes full of defiance before it answered, again in a guttural voice, "She will lure other humans into unholy appetites, and therefore demons will ride them into perdition."

Ema nodded, understanding more than the demon suspected. Then she turned on the evil spirit, and her eyes glowed neon blue, and her voice trembled and echoed around them, "You will not enter this man's body without my permission. If you do, I will take it as an attack on me, and then there is no law that does not allow me to obliterate your existence into beyond nothingness."

The demon in its poor imitation of a living thing crouched before her, and looked away.

The whip in Ema's hand turned solid, and using it as a staff, she drew a circle in the ground, and tapped down once in the center. Blood trickled up from between the drying grass. Kosheen's eyes snapped open, and he sat up. He sniffed the air as his canine teeth lengthened. The snake-like tongue whipped out, feeling the tip of its fangs. He dragged himself over to the pool of blood that swirled around within the circle. He lowered his face and tried to lap it, but an invisible shield prevented it. Kosheen grew frenetic, and then stood up and hissed at Ema, knowing that somehow she did not allow him to drink it.

"As long as you inhabit that body, you cannot taste this sweet blood. Abandon the body, and you can feast upon it."

Kosheen's eyes rolled back in his head until only the whites were visible. The man's body dropped backwards onto the ground like a limp rag; in its place stood a figure that looked similar to Kyle Kosheen. The vampire used the imprint of the last human it inhabited. It fingers were long and misshapen. The feet were those of a bird of prey, and it lacked any sexual organs. The knobs of its vertebrae stuck out of its back giving it a hunchback look. It lunged forward onto all fours to stick its face into the pool of blood. It slurped making grunting noises of satisfaction.

Ema turned the staff in her hand, and it became a spear. The pointed tip glowed white. She came up behind the vampire and with both hands around the shaft, she struck forward and pinned it to the ground, cutting flesh and smashing bone.

The vampire squealed and screamed like a pig being brought to slaughter. The white light that held it in place spread further out from the middle of its body, until its movements slowed down and stopped. With the tip of the spear, Ema picked up the dripping mass of leathery skin and tossed it into the slit that opened into the infinite light beyond. The pool of blood dissipated.

Ander stood guard next to where Jenny lay in the sleeping area of the truck. He stared in mingled awe and terror, at the things that came out of Kyle Kosheen's body. He could not separate himself from the surreal feeling he had stepped into a scene from a horror movie. Then he saw Ema, and it felt like he had found beauty for the first time. He could not understand it, but he recognized this deep desire to protect her at all costs.

Inside his mind, he heard her voice, "Ander, come with the handcuffs, and take this man to the truck."

Ema proved to be right, because he found several handcuffs hidden in the glove compartment. He took one, and walked towards where Ema stood. He observed as multicolored butterflies flew out from the lighted slit in the night's canvas. They floated around her, their wings causing tendrils of a breeze to lift the red cloth wrapped around her body. A large moth with green and aquamarine wings caught the tendrils of her red hair, and held them in place away from her face.

Ander observed the dog thing that lay crouched, with its red eyes trained on the man who moaned on the ground. He could see that its body had become taut with tension, ready to spring at a moment's notice.

Ema said aloud to Ander, "Take him to the truck."

By the white glow coming from the tear, the crouching demon stood up. It looked at Ander as he pulled the man up by the elbows, and handcuffed his hands behind his back. It now looked at the muscled young man as a fleshy bone he could gnaw upon for endless days, but he could not invade one who did not invite him through deed, action or thought.

The demon growled its fury. It no longer controlled its pocket, a human who had committed numerous atrocities at its bidding. The pearly luminescence straying into this world made it desperate to flee into darkness. Ema saw its eyes flit from Ander to the man he instructed in carnage for many years.

True to its nature, it sprung at Kosheen planning to negotiate with Ema after its well-trained pocket became his once again. In that moment, two winged things flew, and tackled Ander to the ground. A bare-chested, scrawny old man with frizzy gray hair stared with round-eyed horror, at what it recognized as the voice that encouraged it in the foulest of deeds. For once, this creature from the darkest pit of hell appeared before him, instead of inside him.

Ema's voice like the holiest bell rang out. "I warned you." She flicked her wrist and the tip of her whip circled around the demon's neck, restraining it from jumping back into Kosheen.

"Human bitch, release me!" it roared.

"As you wish," steely-eyed Ema replied. She jerked the whip hard, decapitating the demon dog known as Scepter. The bloody head rolled towards Ema, and the body fell to the ground twitching in violent bursts. Guts and other internal organs spilled out from the body cavity. A stink more horrible than burning flesh filled the air.

Ander tried to sit up, and found both Duende Fue holding onto his shoulders. They kept muttering about the Sibylline's instructions to keep him safe. He brushed them off and stood up.

He saw as one of the large butterflies that surrounded Ema flew down to the carcass, and from out of its head pulled a pearl of light that pulsed with a steady rhythm. It flew through the tear into the light. The remains of the demon became as ash, and dispersed into the air. The butterflies fluttered with gay abandon around Ema, and then made their way into the place on the other side of the slit, which folded in upon itself and vanished.

Ema stood with arms outstretched. In one hand, she held the whip that shortened, and jumped across into the shield that rested on her other hand. The golden mirror whirled, becoming smaller, and turned once more into a large red rose. The red silken cloth around her body reversed its creation, and once again became a flower. They fell apart, and the petals floated away leaving behind a heavenly scent.

Ema stood naked, and Ander thought to himself that he would never tire of seeing her this way.

She smiled at him, and pointed to the disoriented, handcuffed man who stood looking around him as if he had landed on another planet. Ander grabbed him by the arm, and walked him to the truck

Ema sauntered to the picnic table, pulled on her clothes, and went to where Ander stood. Kyle Kosheen now stood handcuffed to the truck door's mirror.

"How is Jenny?" Ema asked Ander in a low voice.

"She's sleeping. They drugged her up good."

"What address in New Orleans is he headed to?"

Ander pulled himself into the truck to check the digital map. He sat there silent for a moment, and his gut lurched.

"You will not believe this." He said as he stepped down to stand next to Ema.

"Tell me." She said in a low voice.

"The address is Donny's office."

XXI. Ashes

ANDER SAT IN THE RED PICK-UP, STARING at a crazy old guy handcuffed to his truck. Hard to believe he'd been killing people for at least thirty years. Ema sat next to him.

Quiet filled the night. Ander guessed the man stopped his pacing because of the cessation of movement, and then he made out the creak of leather. It came from the back seat area of the truck. He overheard another light scuffle, and turned on the interior light of the cab. They turned around and found both Duende Fue waiting like two kids to be buckled in by their parents.

Amused, Ander turned around and turned off the light. Ema smiled and said, "What do you want?"

"Our reward," both creatures said in union, "we made the machine stop as you commanded."

"Indeed," said Ema thoughtfully, "and a reward you shall have."

Ander felt the scratch of their three, claw-tipped toes scrambling into the front of the truck. They sat on the center console, and looked at Ema with expectant eyes. She leaned back, and told them to be still.

The beasties like dutiful children did as she bid them. She laid a hand on either head, rubbed their foreheads and murmured low words.

"Well, that's done." she announced.

The Duende Fue looked around, and then at Ema. "Where is our reward?" One of them asked scrunching up its face.

"It's yours already."

One Duende Fue turned to the other intending to ask if it understood where the reward had been hidden, then it screeched in horror, "Your eyes, what's wrong with your eyes?"

The other creature stood up with astonishing speed, clicked the button for the light and stared at itself in the rearview mirror. This one cried out in an even louder voice, "My eyes Sibyllina, what have you done? Why are you punishing us?"

Ander made a slight movement, and both Duende Fue turned and glared at him. He looked at their faces, and then put a hand over his mouth to cover a smile.

The creatures stared at him from the loveliest, ultra marine colored eyes. They were large and almond shaped. The needle-like teeth were hard to overlook, but Ander imagined what they looked like when they were only Duendes.

The one standing up, looked again at its reflection with wonder instead of horror. A flicker of recognition crossed its face, and then a tear slipped out of the corner of its eye.

Ema's voice cut across the silence, "If you have any more complaints, I can keep on rewarding you."

The Duende Fue, with a flick of its finger hit the button for the sunroof, and both of them flew off into the night without another word.

Ema took her phone, provided the listener with the location of the rest area and gave instructions for law enforcement to be notified.

She then turned to Ander, "Let's get on the road and pull up ahead on the shoulder. Once we see police coming, we can keep going."

Ander nodded his head, the truck roared to life, and he drove it towards the exit. He parked it on the shoulder, and turned the blinkers on. Not even five minutes passed before blue lights threaded through the traffic from both directions.

Ander pulled the truck back into the road, and looked sideways at Ema, who sat quiet and still next to him.

"Ema, you know that they're bound to find some DNA evidence that belongs to me."

She looked at him and smiled, "No Ander, you have changed because of me. Any DNA traces you left cannot be identified." She paused, and then added, "But now we need to find out what is Donny's part in this."

Ander shifted in his seat, the adrenaline in his body had masked the soreness but now the throbbing in his muscles returned.

"Ema," he explained, "I've known him for several years, but only on a business level. He pays me well, so I can wait between jobs, but I know that his company does several excursions I've never been on."

Ema bit her lips, and then said, "Let's assume he is part of this trafficking ring somehow. Right now, he's aware of the arrest at the warehouse, but he doesn't know we're involved. As far as he's concerned you're still due to come help him by Sunday, for this trip going out into the Gulf."

Ander's voice sounded weary, "We will have to stop, and gas up soon."

A few minutes later, they pulled into a lone gasoline station off an exit. When he went inside to get something to drink, and some pain reliever Ema slipped into the driver seat.

He saw by the stubborn set of her jaw she would not let him drive, so he sat next to her and sighed as he drank water and popped some aspirin. Ten minutes later, he snored softly next to her. Ema drove lost in thought. She rehearsed in her mind how she would tell Ander that he worked for a vampire, which she had pursued for the last two hundred years.

Ema shook Ander by the shoulder. He peered at her out of one eye, squinting against the morning sun. His mouth felt pasty, and he straightened with slow, cautious movements. He looked around him, and saw they were parked next to several shops. Ander groaned when he stepped out of the truck, and he heard bones popping in his shoulders and knees.

Ema eyed him from across the truck's hood. She could tell he wasn't a morning person. "I stopped here so we can get a change of clothing, and some toiletries. Some breakfast wouldn't be bad either."

Ander grunted in reply, then rubbed his face and nodded. She suggested in an amused voice, "Why don't you get us something to eat, and I'll run in there and get the rest of what we need."

He nodded, gave her a thumbs up and ambled towards a coffee shop. Ander stopped, turned around and watched her as she walked across the parking lot. Her swaying hips held him mesmerized, and he mumbled to himself, "Son, you're in big trouble."

Less than half an hour later, they were both sitting in the truck. They drank coffee and ate scrambled eggs and ham from a Styrofoam plate. They made small talk, and none would have suspected what they witnessed in the last twenty-four hours.

Ander drove into New Orleans, and took them to a small bed-and-breakfast named Maison du Sol, located a few blocks from the French Quarter.

Ema had gone to the bathroom to shower when he called Donny, and his assistant Minerva answered the phone. She sounded upset and flustered, and told him in a brusque tone that Donny couldn't take his call. Ander asked in a calm voice what occurred.

Her voice sounded irritated when she answered, "Ander something's happened and Donny's not sure if he'll even be able to take the party out on the Gulf trip."

Ander smiled to himself, "Minerva let him know I'm in New Orleans, and if he plans to call off the trip to notify me right away. I'm sure those guys will be disappointed."

He heard a long silence at the other end, before she said, "You have no idea." Without another word, she hung up.

Ander switched on the television, and the news flashed on a local station. Ema exited the bathroom drying her hair, and with a towel wrapped around her, stood to listen to the reporter who with a serious face discussed the breaking news:

A federal arrest warrant was executed on the owner of the House of Love Flower Distributors for using interstate facilities for racketeering, money laundering and human trafficking of a minor for a commercial sex act. The criminal complaint alleges that Fanny Foster, 39, was arrested in connection with her operation of multiple massage parlors in this state as well as Louisiana, Georgia and Florida. Along with the arrest of Foster on these federal charges, several seizure warrants were also executed on bank accounts linked to the allegations against Foster. Several dozen search warrants are expected to be executed at massage parlors in these states. Seven men and two women, who were also on the premises are believed to run a local prostitution ring, and were arrested. Four underage individuals considered trafficking victims were discovered and taken to an unidentified organization for services and help.

In a separate incident but that law enforcement believes might be connected, Jenny Zhu, 19, who was reported missing three days ago was found drugged in the back of a semi-truck at a rest stop fifty miles from the state line. She was heavily sedated and was tied up. Kyle Earl Kosheen, 67, owner of the truck was found handcuffed to the tractor-trailer's side mirror. He seemed disoriented and unable to explain why the woman was in his truck. Miss Zhu's family owns a business that is located close to the House of Love Flowers. Police believe she was being taken to New Orleans, but the case is under investigation and charges are still pending. Miss Zhu has been reunited with her family and Kyle Kosheen is under arrest and being assessed before his first appearance in court.

Ander muted the volume and turned to Ema, "I called Donny's office and his assistant told me the trip might be called off. Minerva acted bitchier than she usually does. I wonder if this has anything to do with it."

With a raised brow, Ema commented, "It seems coincidental, and you remember what I told you about coincidences, however he has bigger problems than the law."

"He does?" Ander asked with a curious look in his eyes, "What's worse than being arrested as a human trafficker?"

Ema strolled to look out of the second-story window. "I believe that Jenny is the promised sacrifice. Specifically her; that is why he is frenetic right now trying to replace what is irreplaceable. Yes, Donny is in quite a bind." She turned back to Ander, "What can you tell me about him."

"He comes from an old New Orleans family. Pretty well off, and I think he runs this business for the adrenaline, not because he needs the money. He's well connected because we've gone into countries that usually close their doors to outsiders. I know he has an inner circle of clients that have been coming to him for years. I've never been on any of those trips, and I've seen that Donny takes great pains to keep the details of those excursions under wrap."

"Well, let's see who's comes to us. I have a feeling Donny will soon make an appearance."

He winked at her broadly, "So can I talk to you into going to dinner with me at this great Creole restaurant?"

"I am yours to command." She replied with a smile.

The sun dipped into the horizon as they walked to the French Quarter. They found a small, informal restaurant filled with a local crowd.

Ander placed an order for an appetizer, and then noticed small fangs protruding from under the upper lip of their young waitress. She had short hair, dyed purple with burgundy tips. Thin as a rail, and dressed all in black he guessed she considered herself a vampire. Her nametag read 'Jolie'.

When Ema looked up, and told her she wanted an order of jumbo gulf shrimp, the girl just stared at her.

"Are you okay?" Ander reached out to steady her as she swayed on her feet.

"Sorry, I felt this dizzy spell there for a minute." She turned back to Ema and said sheepishly, "I had this feeling like I've seen you before. Probably, somebody that looks like you. I'll be right back with your order."

Ander and Ema noticed throughout the meal that Jolie kept looking at Ema, trying not to be obvious about it. Towards the end of the meal, she approached them.

"I think I remember where I've seen you. I mean somebody that looks like you."

Ema nodded, and asked, "Who do I look like?"

Jolie crouched down so her conversation with them could not be overheard. "I'm an archaeology student down at the university, and about three months ago we were asked to look over some artifacts found in an old house. The estate belonged to the Figueroa family who built it in 1795 as a sugar plantation, while the Spanish held New Orleans. The family estate donated it to the university a few years back, and they finally got around to inspecting it. They discovered a hidden room in the attic behind a false wall."

At this point Jolie's eyes glistened, and she looked at Ema with eyes rounded with wonderment. "They found some neat stuff in the attic that looked like it sat sealed up for at least two hundred years. However, what blew the professor's socks off has to do with this portrait found in a hidden alcove. It's titled in French and Spanish, La Dame Rouge or La Dama Roja which translates to The Red Lady."

She pointed her finger at Ema, "And you're a dead ringer for her. I mean minus the 18th century clothing and that stuff, but wow. I wanted to apologize when I almost passed out, but you see I'm an energy vampire, and you've got waves of it coming off you. I wasn't prepared for that."

Ema listened to her with raised eyebrows. "That's a great story Jolie."

"Is your family from New Orleans? I mean maybe you're descended from her."

"No I am not originally from here." Ema said drily, "So where is this painting at now?"

"It's at the university. The department head is getting it cleaned, which is a slow process, but he's like in seventh heaven because he says there's quite a story tied into this Red Lady dating back to the Renaissance, or even medieval times."

Ander interrupted her, "So how's she tied to the Figueroa family, does anyone know?"

Warming up to her story Jolie continued, "Well the professor explained they were an ancient and aristocratic Spanish family with a troubling history. There were even whispers of heresy. One day someone slaughtered the entire family, all except the eldest son Don Ambrosio Figueroa y Mujica. Secrecy surrounded the motive or identity of the killer. The Church sealed their castle, and ordered the families who lived in the nearby village to move away. They were under penalty of death if they returned to the area. King Charles IV exiled Don Ambrosio to the New World. First, he went to Cuba, and before the year ended, the governor ordered him out of Havana. That's how he ended up here."

"Did he marry this mysterious lady?" Ander asked intrigued by her story.

"No, on the contrary, rumors circulated she came to fulfill a vendetta mission. Some said the Vatican sent her. Others claimed she obeyed the bidding of a powerful European family. That's why she's known as The Red Lady. And get this, in the painting she's got this red dress on, and then with the red hair, no one is sure what the symbolism is beyond the obvious."

Ema stayed quiet. Ander asked, "Who painted her?"

"No one knows. Part of the mystery is the identity of the artist. It turns out that soon after her arrival the young Don Ambrosio vanished from New Orleans. She stayed on at the house for the next twenty years, and after a yellow fever epidemic, she's gone too. Not long afterwards, another Figueroa arrives from Spain, takes over the plantation and it's stayed in the family all this time. Great story, huh?"

Ema looked at Jolie with hooded eyes, "Fascinating."

"Well, I gotta get back to work. I'll ask my professor if there's anything else about the story I left out. You can stop by tomorrow. My name is Jolie O'Malley."

She stepped away and kept looking at Ema. "Man, I can't get over how much you look like her."

XXII. Painted From Memory

ANDER AND EMA MEANDERED down the sidewalk, walking among the throngs of people who walked, talked and shopped in the French Quarter. They found a small outdoor café and sat at a table. Ema suspected that Ander bubbled with questions, and didn't know where to start, so she did it for him.

"Yes, this is how Divine Order works. When it's been disrupted, it will vibrate to bring about circumstances and persons to right the sequence of events. This explains how we go eat at a restaurant where the server connects Donny to a strange family history."

Ander contemplated her as she spoke, and he looked down and then asked her, "Are you the Red Lady?"

"Yes." she answered simply.

Ander went through dozens of questions in a few seconds, but he asked the most pressing one, "Is Donny's family the one who owned the property donated to the university?"

"Yes, but Ander there really isn't a Figueroa family. There is only one member and his name is Donny, or as he was known when he came from Spain, Don Ambrosio Figueroa y Mujica."

Ander stayed quiet, thinking about what she said. "Ema you will have to help me out here."

"Ander he's a vampire. The Donny you know is the same person who arrived at the end of 18th century in New Orleans. What Jolie described is accurate. They were powerful grandees, but suspected of dabbling in the occult. Even the Inquisitors turned a deaf ear to the rumors that were whispered about them. Suspicion swirled around Donny being complicit in the death of his family; however, he came from a noble family, and the royal court wanted to avoid the scandal. The New World promised a solution."

Ema paused, "I came pursuing him and he caught wind of my arrival and disappeared. I stayed behind because New Orleans kept me very busy in those years, and I hoped he would return. I never realized that painting existed until now. Brother Clemente would have known how upset it would make me, which is why I think he hid it."

Ander interrupted her, "Why didn't Donny recognize you when he came to the house?"

"Because, he never saw me. I think my ship docked, and within hours, he left New Orleans on his speediest horse. This suits our purpose now. I also tested him when he came to your house."

"You tested him?"

"Yes, he couldn't come inside until I invited him."

"You mean that's true about vampires?"

"Yes, that is true about many evil entities; they cannot enter without an invitation."

Ander reviewed everything he saw in the movies about vampires. "How can he move about in daytime?"

"He is an old vampire, and I am sure that sometimes he stays indoors, or comes out only after dark."

"If he's such an old vampire, what would he be afraid of? You said that because he lost Jenny, he's in a bind."

"Well as evil as Donny is, he's currying favor from something more evil than himself. There is great risk in dishonoring a blood promise."

"What do you think he'll try to do?"

"Survive. He is in danger of being the sacrifice himself. He must come up with a substitute."

"Ema what would be a substitute for Jenny? Another girl?"

"No, it doesn't have to be another woman; it could be someone who doesn't expect to be sacrificed. There is something that pleases these dark beings, when they bring humans who do not understand they are the intended victim."

Ander's phone rang. Donny apologized about the delay, and told Ander the trip would take place. He wanted to know if he would meet the captain of the ship at a nearby bar. Ander agreed.

They walked a few blocks and stepped into a smoky, ill-lit dive. In the corner, an overweight man with a short ponytail waved them over, and greeted them heartily as they sat in two empty stools. The thick odor of beer hung like a cloud over him.

"You must be Ander, I'm Captain Oliver."

"I heard that maybe the trip would be canceled."

The man took a gulp of beer, and cleaned his lips with his shirtsleeve. "Naw man, Donny told me to he can't go because he's got business to take care of, but there's no need to cancel the entire trip."

Captain Oliver's eyes settled on Ema, and he looked her up and down. "Are you going?" he asked bluntly.

"No, I'm not." she answered him shortly.

"Well you should, I think you'd have a great time." His eyes became a little unfocused.

He turned back to Ander. "You know I don't know why Donny needs you in on this, no offense."

Ander waved his hand, dismissing his concern.

"Do you know how many times I've been out with these old bastards? Nothing will happen."

Ander shrugged his shoulders, and offered a plausible excuse, wondering himself why Donny called him. "He's being a cautious businessman. Nobody wants to get sued."

"Sued?" the old man snorted. "None of those guys would sue. Do you know how much dirt Donny has on them? Naw, I think since he's sitting this one out, he wants them to feel like they're in safe hands."

Captain Oliver then peered at both of them, hiccupped and asked them if they wanted a beer. Ema and Ander both shook their heads. He signaled for the waiter to bring him another one.

His eyes lit up, "I remember now, why he is in such a god-damned hurry for us to talk. He moved up the date of departure to tomorrow. My crew is ready, the clients are here and they have no problem getting extra days on the trip for the same fee."

He looked at Ander with bleary eyes. "You know I think you're right. Donny wants to write on some piece of paper that you and I spoke, and we discussed my medical knowledge." He tried to wink his eye, but it resulted only in a loss of equilibrium. He almost fell face forward into the table.

Ander steadied him until he sat upright again. "So Captain I heard you're taking them to fish for marlin and tuna."

The man nodded his head. "Yep, but you know every once in a while some pretty little mermaids show up, and that's when the partying really starts. Man if the walls of that yacht could talk." He leered, and made another attempt at a wink that almost put him under the table.

Ema asked in a soft voice, "What's the name of your boat?"

"Alcyone."

Captain Oliver turned to Ander, "So are we square? We talked right?"

"Yes, you could say that."

"Perfect. I think I'll have another beer, and head out. They're transporting provisions out to the yacht as we speak, and we're leaving with the morning tide."

Ander and Ema took a deep breath of the odor-free air outside the bar. Ema took Ander by the arm, and walked him away down the sidewalk.

She gazed at him because she expected that he would be unhappy with her next words. "I need to go somewhere, that you cannot accompany me." She put up her hand forestalling his words. "It's because you would be in grave danger, and I'll explain later, but I think the best thing would be for you to go back to the bed-and-breakfast and wait for me there. If Donny calls, and asks you to meet him, stall but do not go to where he's at."

Ander put his hands on his hips and looked down. The plan did not make him happy. "Where are you going?" he asked.

"To Jackson Square, across from the cathedral."

Then a caw sounded behind him, and Ander turned around to see a large white gull watching them both. It perched on a chartreuse-colored, wooden fence that enclosed an inner courtyard for a restaurant.

He looked back at Ema, and said, "I know by now that this gull is not here, because it has nowhere else to be."

Ema smiled as she walked up to the bird that looked steadily at her, and ruffled its feathers. He observed her whisper something to it, and then it flew off into the dark skies.

"I will be back soon." She turned and melted into the crowds, and then down one of the side streets that led away from the bright lights of the shops and restaurants."

Ander's eyes followed her retreating figure until she disappeared from sight. He stretched feeling his muscles pull painfully. This wait-in-the-room scenario did not suit him, but he realized he had no other choice. He walked down the sidewalk, and then turned down a wide alley that ran between the old buildings. It took him to a parking lot where employees of several of the businesses parked their car. There were dumpsters lined up against a back wall. A myriad of odors came from them.

Ander walked along, part of him worried about Ema then, he discerned a whimper. The dim lighting made it hard to see, and then the dull boom of something thumping against one of the metal dumpsters carried across the parking lot. He turned and walked in that direction, several cars blocking the view. A full-throated scream ended in a squeal.

He sprinted a few feet further, and saw a figure holding someone down against a bin. The person underneath flailed their legs, and a hand covered their mouth. The assailant engrossed in holding down his victim, did not hear Ander come up behind him. He grabbed the attacker by the collar, and threw him a few feet away.

Ander looked down, and saw the tear-streaked face of Jolie O'Malley. He saw her eyes tracking a person coming up behind him. He turned rapidly, and struck the man a vicious blow to the chin. The attacker staggered back, and Ander circled around him. He feinted a blow to the left, which left the assailant's face uncovered, and then he hit him in the mouth, jolting the man's teeth. He shook his head, and came in fast. Ander still stiff, caught a blow to the right side of his face. He tried to hit Ander in the body, but he ducked his head against the man's shoulder and spun him off balance before hitting him in the belly. Then he stepped back, and punched him hard twice in the head.

Faint shouts alerted the assailant that others were running towards them. He ducked behind some cars, and Ander saw him vault over a fence. He turned around to where Jolie still sat against the dumpster, and offered her a hand up. She wiped tears from her dirt-smudged face.

Two busboys from the nearby restaurant ran up. Jolie assured them that nothing happened to her. They turned around, and shook Ander's hand. Jolie said no police should be called, but she'd appreciate it if they would walk her back to her workplace.

Before leaving with them, she caught Ander by the arm and said in a trembling voice, "Thanks for what you did but I think you should know about this."

Ander wiped his perspiring face and said, "Tell me."

"He kept asking about the portrait, and calling her La Dama de Sangre, which I know enough Spanish to understand means, The Lady of Blood. I said the last I knew the university had it."

She lowered her voice "I told him no, and I think he would have killed me." Then she gulped and looked into Ander's eyes. "He had fangs, like me," and touched the tips of her sharpened teeth with her finger. " I know all the vampires in New Orleans, and he's not one of them. I know I offered to find out more about it, but do me a favor and don't come looking for me. I'm sorry, but there's evil surrounding that portrait."

She walked to where the two teenagers waited for her, and they made their way down the alley and melted into the murky light between the buildings.

Ander flexed his hands, and looked down to see blood coming from his barely-healed knuckles. He looked around him, knowing someone watched their every move. Once Donny saw the portrait, Ema's secret would be known. He changed direction, and headed towards Jackson Square.

XXIII. The Unburied

EMA MADE HER WAY DOWN THE STONE steps that brought her to the turgid waters of the Mississippi River. Far off tinny music carried across the distance The wayward whiff of spiced food hung fresh upon the breeze. Behind her rose the towers of St. Louis Cathedral.

The park had already closed when Ema arrived which suited her purpose. She cloaked herself in a glamour of invisibility to keep her hidden from curious eyes. At the edge of the steps that led to the water's edge she knelt down. Her hand slipped into the cool liquid. Something fluttered against her skin and then a webbed hand grabbed hers, and a delft-colored face broke the surface of the water. Large silver eyes dominated her features, and a mouth full of sharp teeth sat below a small slit of a nose. Grayish green hair hung over her shoulders, and fell back into the water. Pieces of coral, seaweed and small marine animals nestled among her tresses.

"You summoned me sister." A sibilant whisper came from the mermaid.

"There is a boat named the Alcyone that is leaving on the morning tide. They will travel out far in the Gulf to capture large fish. It will be filled with men who are not intended to return, but only to serve the purpose of one who is my enemy. You will help me and in exchange, you can have their sweet flesh to feast upon."

In Ema's open palm, a green cube pulsed. "This holds the essence of one of them, so you may find the vessel. Will you take them?"

The creature pulled herself up. The strong scent of the sea clung to her shiny blue skin. Her full breasts had no nipples, and below the hips iridescent scales gleamed. The mermaid's tail, like a fan splashed quietly behind her.

She nodded, and took the green cube and put it into her mouth. She then put her hand on Ema's cheek. It felt cool, but vibrant with life that coursed through it. "Come with me sister," she whispered.

"I cannot. Your place is there, this is mine." Ema turned her face and kissed the mermaid's palm. "You have only to call on me, and I will come to you." She whispered back.

The mermaid bowed her head, and then passed a hand over her face, when she looked up her features were beautiful, almost breathtaking in their perfection. She floated backwards, and then sank into the water, her floating hair the last vestiges of her presence.

Ema turned around, and climbed the stone steps leading into Jackson Square. She saw several men milling about at the gate into the park. Their faces were blank, and they answered a call they were unable to resist. Some women clung to their arms, trying to pull them back but without success. They would not respond to questions or threats.

Ema passed through the small crowd that gathered as the spell broke, and the men blinked their eyes as someone who has awoken from a deep sleep. She set her steps towards the bed-and-breakfast when Ander walked up to her. She looked at him and guessed that something occurred.

Before she asked, he blurted out, "Donny knows that you're the woman in the portrait."

Ema stood still, calculating in her mind what would be her next steps, because the success of her plan hinged on this.

"How do you know this?"

"I came across Jolie being attacked behind the restaurant. She told me the man wanted to know where to find the portrait. The man had fangs like her, but she doesn't recognize him from the vampires that live in New Orleans."

Ema looped her arms through Ander, and they strolled along in the humid night.

"Ema," Ander said in alarm, "how would anyone know what we spoke about, or to whom if we're not being followed? Jolie also said he kept asking about the Lady of Blood, but in Spanish."

They stopped walking, and he looked at her with troubled eyes.

"That's you right?" he asked.

"Yes."

"Why would you be known by that name?"

"Because I hunted many vampires at that time, and they weren't energy vampires."

Ema then pulled his face into the light of a nearby lamp, and she saw the dried blood on his cheekbone. "Who did this?" she asked coldly.

"The son of a bitch who attacked Jolie, we traded a few punches and then he ran off."

"There's one place we have to go to now."

"To the university?"

"The painting is not there. It's at the place where the restorer works from."

Once inside the pick-up, Ander pulled out his phone and looked for anyone who worked on restoration projects of fine art pieces.

Ema put her hand over his arm. "Wait." She said. "Donny is pressed for time. He cannot delay another twenty-four hours to break in, and get this painting."

Ander scrolled through different sites. "There's a few of them in the city."

"Is there one that specializes in restoring old portraits?"

"Yes, a woman named Celine Scarso. It looks like she 's worked with the university before on other projects."

"Let's go there."

Ander headed towards the address showed on the website. He looked at Ema and asked her, "What do you mean he doesn't have time to break in?"

"He will influence her to bring it to him, and he will do it tonight."

They came to a narrow street, lined with older wooden houses some of them painted in bright colors. They sat on brick foundations and their proximity to the sidewalk testified to how long ago they were built. Many of the structures were converted to business use, and a few vehicles were parked along the street. They came to a corner where a street lamp spread a pool of light underneath it. Ema looked at Ander's face, and saw that he stared at a point further up the road..

"What is it?" she asked.

"I don't fucking believe it." he exclaimed. Brakes throbbed as Ander pulled the red pick-up short, turned the corner and parked.

He turned to Ema, "I just saw Minerva, Donny's assistant, get out of her car. She's about half way up the block."

Ema spoke in hurried tones. "If you approach Minerva, she'll recognize you. The woman turning over the painting will wake up tomorrow with a terrible headache, and no clue of what happened to the portrait. I'm sure I can get Minerva to cooperate. Let me borrow your phone."

Ander raised his brow in doubt, and handed over the cellular. "That lady is a piece of work. Be careful, she's vicious." Ema slid from the truck, and noiselessly closed the door.

She rounded the corner of the street, and strolled along seemingly engrossed in a conversation on her phone. Further down, she saw two women standing behind an SUV with its hatch door open, one of them pivoted and glared at Ema.

Minerva saw a tall woman with a long ponytail, wearing jeans, sneakers and a sky blue top. A phone to her ear, she appeared engrossed in a conversation. An airheaded artist she assumed.

Next to her Celine Scarso stood with a vacant look in her eyes. The portrait covered by a cloth lay in the carpeted trunk area.

The overweight woman, named Minerva Mata, balled her hand into a fist. Dark, blotchy skin contrasted with her badly permed, blonde hair, and beads of moisture dotted her upper lip. She lived in a constant state of rage, which simmered at the best of times, or like now felt ready to explode. An unexpected witness created quite a problem for her.

Minerva looked up and down the block, and didn't see anyone else. She mulled over the thought of mowing the woman down, but she remembered that Donny warned her about no messes. What if she gave her a hard knock on the head, and took her back to the office?

She thought to herself, "That's not a bad idea."

The woman approached her with a goofy grin, and she in turn put on her nice, middle-age woman dressed in polyester look. Her hand furtively grabbed a police baton she kept next to some jumper cables.

She raised her other hand, waved and said a cheery, "Hi."

The woman with the red hair made a b-line for her, waving her hand like an idiot. She put the phone in her back pocket, and said to the silent figure next to her, "Hey Celine, what's up?"

Minerva tightened her grip on the baton, and swung it over her head. She felt a vise-like grip around her wrist that caused pain to shoot up her arm.

She stared in horror at the artsy-bohemian looking lady whose eyes glimmered with a blue light.

"Naughty, naughty girl." The woman whispered to her in a voice that made her squirt shit into her underwear. She dropped the baton, and it clunked on the street.

The woman turned to Celine. "I want you to go inside your home, and you'll remember nothing about me, or seeing this woman before. In five minutes you will call the police, and tell them that there's a woman at the corner stripping off her clothing and screaming she's going to kill someone, make sure to mention she has a gun."

Celine nodded, opened the gate to her yard, trudged to her home and went inside.

Ema went around to the side of the vehicle, dragging Minerva along and opened the passenger side door. The woman's purse slumped carelessly on the seat; inside a .38 revolver sat nestled among some white tissue. Minerva's piggish eyes bugged out of her head, because she feared this person more than she did Donny. Hell, even Donny feared her.

"It's time for your close-up." Ema said, grabbing Minerva by her hair. She shook her a few times, and then she flicked her on the forehead. The woman's face became flaccid, and Ema wrinkled her nose at the stench of feces coming from her. The woman stood with her arms hanging to her side.

"Minerva, you will go to the corner and strip off your clothes; wave this gun around and say you want to kill someone. Do not drop this gun no matter what the police tell you to do. When they take you in, you will not cooperate and when you speak to the doctor, I want you to tell him every horrible thing you've done, and then confess to the police as well."

Ema handed her the gun , "Off you go." She pushed her toward the direction of the four-way stop sign. The chubby woman sauntered to the corner, screaming and stripping off clothing at the same time.

With the painting in hand, Ema walked back to where Ander waited with the truck running. He pulled out as soon as she closed the door. They went down the block, and turned on a busy street that led back to the French Quarter. A police cruiser passed them traveling in the opposite direction, then stopped, turned on its lights and did a u-turn. It raced off toward where they left Minerva.

Once back in their room, Emma explained, "Donny promised a sacrifice, and he knows he cannot fulfill it. Do you wonder why he decided after all to send out the fishing party, even a few days earlier?"

Ander nodded, "Yes, I thought Donny would be on the next flight to a country with no extradition agreements with the United States."

"Ander, what will come for him is much worse than the law, and it doesn't care about borders or extradition laws. He knows it. His plan is to send out those men, the clients and the crew, as a replacement for the victim he lost. He's hoping to buy some time, and in a practical sense, it ties up loose ends for him. Authorities can never question a past client or someone that worked for him about his activities, if they're dead. My guess is he'll send someone out to intercept them and chuck them overboard, but that's after they've been tortured for a few hours as part of the sacrifice ceremony."

"What do you think he'll do with the time he buys, go after Jenny again?"

"He will not be buying any time because there will be no sacrifice. Those men will belong to someone else, and take my word for it; it'll be a fitting end."

Ander's somber voice asked, "How long does that demon delay in coming for its sacrifice?"

"No time at all."

Ander's eyes turned to the portrait, still wrapped and waiting on the table. "Shall we?" he asked.

Ema nodded.

Ander pulled off the covering, and studied the figure on the canvas. Ema wearing a deep red, empire dress stared back at him. She sat in an armless chair, and the simplicity of her toga style gown contrasted with the jewel-like tones used to paint her. A yellow shawl draped across her legs. The red hair, unadorned and pinned up framed her face. The artist captured the green gray of her eyes, which stared directly at the observer. A half smile played on her lips.

Ander looked at the painting, and then back at Ema. "You look beautiful." He said.

"Thank you." she whispered.

"You look like you stepped out of one of those romantic, English mini-series." He turned the painting around and an intricate cursive script spelled out, La Dame Rouge, underneath it, La Dama Roja, and the date May 1, 1800.

"Ema, who painted this? It could only be someone who knew you well."

She sighed. "You remember I mentioned the name of Brother Clemente? Clemente Figueroa y Mujica, the youngest son of the Figueroa family, is the young monk that accompanied me. His family insisted that he take holy orders, in hopes that he would become a prince of the Church. They did not consider his desire to be an artist. He had no choice but to obey. Inadvertently they saved his life. He lived in a monastery, when his parents and sisters were killed. Brother

Clemente came with me to clear his brother or redeem him, and could do neither."

"What happened to him?" Ander asked.

"During the 1820s another fever epidemic ran through New Orleans. One day while he worked in the city aiding those who died, he saw his brother. When he told me, I realized that among so many dead, those being killed by a vampire would not merit special attention. He feasted on healthy humans."

Ema paced back and forth, as she remembered those days, "Clemente became obsessed with finding his brother. He wanted to save him. He did not understand what he battled, and that his brother reveled voluntarily in the grip of great evil. They found his body drained of blood, close to the cathedral where he ministered to the poor."

Ander asked, "Was he your pocket?"

Ema smiled at his curiosity, "No, and one day soon I will tell you the story of why I left New Orleans after Clemente's death."

XXIV. Red Delirium

THE NEXT MORNING ANDER AWOKE alone. Then something shifted inside of him, and he discerned the murmur of her voice in his brain. Soon after, he forgot about her presence.

He took a shower, and went to have breakfast at a small café. He sat engrossed in thought as he ate an order of beignet with a café au lait. Meanwhile, he waited for a call from Donny but none came. Ander admitted to himself that he felt relieved. He kept reviewing all his interactions with Donny throughout the years, wondering what clue he missed. Donny disappeared for months on end, but he attributed it to expeditions that took him out of the country. His unusual request about scouting out the wildlife park fired dark suspicions in him. Did he walk into a perfect setup, so he would be an easy prey for that werewolf thing?

He watched television, and then slept throughout the afternoon. Shadows walked across the wall ahead of the setting sun. He finally sat up, and his stomach grumbled with hunger. Ema stared at him from across the room.

"Hungry?" she asked.

He nodded, and got dressed. Ema told him to take everything because they would not return to the room.

They found another small restaurant within walking distance. While they ate, the light outside faded and they stepped out into the night, blending into the tourists and locals who meandered through the streets of the French Quarter. They peered into shop windows, as they made their way to where the truck waited for them.

Flashing blue lights from police cars greeted them when they arrived at their destination. A yellow tarp covered a body that lay on the street next to their pick up. The police tried to stop them, but they showed their room key, and they were allowed to walk further in. They stood next to a small crowd made up of the other guests.

Ander asked a middle-aged man standing next to him what happened.

"Some guy screamed. He went down, and died before hitting the ground. I heard the cops comment that maybe he took some bad drugs. He's young, and get this, he's one of these kids that put on those fake fangs. What a dumb ass." The man shook his head and walked off

It must have been a slow night for homicides because the medical examiner's office showed up within thirty minutes to transport the body to their office; soon after the police left, removing most of the yellow tape.

Ema and Ander walked to the truck. Ander stared at a dusty palm print next to the handle of the door. The body had lain only a few feet below it.

Ema commented to him in a matter-of-fact way, "I'm not forgiving of thieves. I'm sure Donny experienced a tremor when his little minion was dissolved. He's getting messy, which means he's getting desperate."

"Won't that corpse be sneaking out of the ME's office later tonight?"

"No, I doubt it. Despite being more human than vampire, he shared one of their weaknesses already."

"Which is?"

"Holy or consecrated items in any form are lethal."

Their conversation ended when a white gull landed on the hood of the truck. It looked at Ema, stretched out its wings, cawed once and flew off.

She turned to Ander, "Where is Donny's office?"

"Not too far from here. He converted a Victorian townhouse, and he lives on the top floor.

Ander deftly maneuvered the truck through traffic, until they turned down a tree-lined avenue with beautiful, restored homes. They came to one that sat on a corner lot. A balcony with intricate cast-iron railings, and louvered shutters run across the length of the second story; below it granite steps led to a recessed door.

Ema and Ander stood in front of the house, and felt the oppressive gloom that emanated from it. They discerned a soft clacking sound, and followed it to the side of the property. An unlatched garden gate moved in the soft, humid breeze. Inside they found a courtyard dominated by a low, brick enclosure. A lion's head spouted water into a pool below, that reflected the night sky. The gurgling sound of the water dominated the silence.

Out of a wedge of darkness in the corner, Donny stepped out into the light cast by an antique style lamp that hung on a pole.

"We meet at last, Sibyllina." Ander saw long fangs grow as he spoke. For the first time he realized Donny looked like Chris Sarandon, the vampire in the movie *Fright Night*.

"That sounds so contrived, doesn't it?" Donny asked in his normal voice.

"Let's try it again."

"What do you want bitch?" he said in a low guttural growl.

Ema looked at him again with an impassive face. She finally answered him in measured tones. "It's not what I want, it what he wants." and pointed behind her. She took Ander's arm, and pulled him away.

A tall figure, dressed in a brown monk's robe stood in the opening of the doorway. The hood drawn over the face exposed only the lower jaw. Around its waist, it wore a rope that ended in what looked like a shrunken, human head.

Ander gagged when the fetidness that came with the figure hit him. It advanced in, and fear crossed Donny's face.

The noise emitted by the figure heralded an antithesis to a place that abounded in life. It existed only in a place sterile and dead. Long teeth, and longer fangs sprouted from its mouth. As it stepped, a hollow echo sounded within the vacuum that came with its presence.

"Don Ambrosio Figueroa y Mujica, I have come for my tribute."

"You have not found favor with the men I have sent to you? I will reclaim the girl, and bring her to you with my own hands."

"If I was satisfied would I be here?"

"The men..."

The snarl that rippled from the creature silenced Donny, "What men? What blood, what prize have you given me? There is nothing, except you."

The hooded figure pointed to Donny with a hand tipped with long black nails.

"These were my hunting grounds long before you came, and I allowed you a place to slake your thirst with the agreement that you would give me my due."

The creature curled its fingers inward, and Donny's body curved towards it, as if pulled by invisible hooks. Ander looked with horrified fascination, and realized that human fingers decorated a necklace it wore around its neck. Large flies buzzed around the bits of plump flesh that oozed blood.

Donny growled back at the thing, fury filling his face. He could not call himself master any longer. It hissed at the tall figure and asked, "What do you want? A larger tribute, more lives, more souls? I will serve you and fulfill whatever task you ask of me."

The demon threw its head back, and made noises that were anything but mirthful. "Servant or slave, I need neither of these. What I want is suffering, and it's not only living things that experience agony."

It grabbed Donny by the neck and brought him into its embrace, before biting him deeply on the side of the face and drawing out blood, which fell in puddles below their feet. Donny screamed in exquisite pain, and his body shuddered.

"This is the first of my many kisses so you will understand how profoundly you are now mine. You will always be mine. I sense a deep well of misery that I will pull agony from for all eternity."

The thing called Donny whimpered, as the demon vampire held him by his hair before him.

It then turned its gaze on Ema, and Ander who stood in a corner of the courtyard. "You have won the day, crafty Sibyllina. I have no choice, but to take one that has brought me countless bodies and souls through the years. I know your hand has wrought his destruction. I will not forget."

Ema clapped her hands once, and a sharp discordance like a crack of thunder rent the silence. Ander slammed against the wall of the house as a well of light opened under Ema's feet, and she now stood clothed in a deep red armor that hugged her body, arms and legs. She advanced on the creature, and caught it under its throat.

"What will you not forget?" her voice sounded like a glass bell.

She shook the vampire as a dog shakes a rat. It dropped the remnants of Donny on the ground and its hood fell back. It became shorter, and the teeth shrank back, the miasma dispersed. What Ema held by the neck had become an old monk with a white beard and a tonsured head.

"I will tell you what you will not forget." she said in a terrible voice. "I am the Lady in Red, I am the Lady of Blood. I have hunted vampires and worse through the ages. I will be the one now to mete out punishment. I condemn you both to exist in the light of all lights, where there is no shadow, or deception and you may think on how you came to be where you are."

Ema pulled out a net that glowed with a golden light from a small bag on her waist. She threw it first over Donny who cried out in agony when the fibers touched his body, and his skin smoked as if scorched. He hissed at Ema with drawn back lips, his withered features unrecognizable. She threw the old man into the net, which enlarged to accommodate him, and he screamed out. His face once again became cadaverous and his fangs crew as he writhed inside the golden confines.

Where the gate of the garden stood, a tall figure entered bathed in a pearly, white light that sparkled in all colors, but none at the same time. Tall and hooded, it held out its arms, its exact features were indistinct. Ema threw the net to it, and as it grabbed the squirming vampires, it fell backwards and melted away, the light winking out into nothing.

XXV. Blue Side of the Rip Line

THE LUXURY YACHT BOBBED IN THE GULF waters. The seas were calm and reflected the early morning sky where a few white clouds passed overhead. No sounds came from the ship.

This is what two men that boarded her detected immediately. They were hit men hired to dispatch all onboard, but they found no one to kill. They checked each luxurious stateroom with drawn pistols. The Jacuzzi tub bubbled, and two pair of men's lounge slippers sat discarded on the edge. There were cut vegetables on a slice board in the kitchen, all in preparation for a meal left uncooked. The bedrooms showed signs of occupancy; men's clothing on the bed or luggage in the closet. The crew's quarters were empty. A soccer match played on the television.

The two men met again on the aft deck after clearing the ship, and looked at each with the same result: the ship had no passengers or crew. An overpowering, fish market smell lay like an unseen miasma over the boat.

Their instructions were clear: kill everyone on board, including the crew, by gaining access to the ship with the pretense of delivering girls. The two men scanned the horizon, and only a solitary gull hovered overhead. The speedboat they arrived on beckoned with a silent invitation to leave as soon as possible. Neither of them could deny the disquiet that flooded their gut urging them to head back to dry land.

A solitary, hard splash sounded out. They both drew their pistols again; one walked with a measured tread towards the space between the ships, and as a precaution, the other one went to the opposite side of the yacht.

One named Rice looked cautiously over the side. His eyes widened when he saw an angelic face staring up at him from the water. Her blonde hair floated around her, and she stretched an arm up in supplication. Under normal circumstances, he would have been suspicious, no matter how beautiful the woman, but the desire to embrace her flooded his brain. When his body plunged into the sea, webbed hands grabbed his legs and dragged him under. The trail of air bubbles coming from him fizzled out.

The other man called out to his companion after hearing the splash. The expected reply did not come, and a deep-rooted instinct warned him not to look for his companion. He saw a shadow swim just under the surface of the water, and disappear under the ship. The movement of its large tail looked mammalian, like a dolphin. A hard man, he could not deny the fear that twined around his spine, spawned by superstitions he rarely thought of as an adult. He remembered stories his Greek grandmother told him about mermaids; not a Disney princess or a male fantasy with double-Ds, but ones who captured sailors and fishermen and ate them.

He dug under his shirt and fingered a square-sided cross, made of iron that he wore around his neck held by a leather thong. He pulled it with a rough tug, and clutched it tightly inside a meaty fist. He made a running leap down onto the deck of the boat that awaited him. The assassin looked neither right nor left as he untied the rope that bound the vessels together. The motor roared to life, and he eased the vessel away from the side and then sped up. Before he lost sight of the yacht, he turned and looked over his shoulder. Two women hung onto the anchor line. One of them waved a hand in farewell. He furtively turned his face away, and pushed the boat to an even greater speed.

The Coast Guard came across the deserted ship several days later, and immediately towed it back to shore. Inquiries made as to the owner of the ship led back to Donny Figueroa. The FBI opened an investigation based on a confession made by Minerva Mata, a strange woman held in the county psych ward. Using the information she provided, they went to question Donny, however it seemed the earth had swallowed him. Several weeks would pass before they realized the connection between several missing person's reports, and this case. It seemed that several well-connected businessmen had gone missing all at the same time. The fate of the crew also remained a mystery.

XXVI. High Strangeness

ANDER DRAPED HIS SHIRT OVER EMA'S naked body.

"So this is what happens to your clothes when you don't take them off first?"

Ema nodded, "Yes, they practically sizzle off my skin, and it's placed me in many compromising situations through the years. I try to avoid it when I can, but sometimes that's not an option."

Ander guided Ema out of the side gate of Donny's property. The truck waited close by on the curb. An older lady walking her cocker spaniel looked at Ema's bare legs, then at Ander's naked chest and crossed the street to the other sidewalk.

Ander headed towards the highway that would take them back to D'Etchepare. Once they left the city behind, Ander turned to Ema.

"I don't know what to ask you about what happened."

Ema smiled at him. "Ander you can ask as many questions as you wish, and I understand that so much has been thrown at you in a short amount of time."

Ander nodded his head, and said, "Let's start with Donny. He's a vampire, and he's been around for over two hundred years. How did he get away with no one asking questions?"

"He's always hired people to manage the day to day so he need not make an appearance. Once it became noticeable that he wasn't aging, he would move away for a few years. He then reintroduces himself as a nephew or other relative left as the heir by the previous Donny. Persons who were familiar with the prior incarnation, have moved away or died, or see what they expect to see, a relative that has a striking family resemblance. He can invent a new identity easily with the wealth he wields."

Ander looked at the road, and then glanced back at Ema. "What about that vampire, or whatever he was, that turned into a monk?"

Ema sighed before answering. "Tomasino, a Capuchin friar came with the first wave of priests sent to the Louisiana Territory to establish missions in the 1720s. Poverty, suffering and ignorance of religion held sway in the land. I suspect him of being a vampire before he came to Louisiana. He preyed on the Indians, and I believe a powerful shaman or medicine man couldn't kill him, but stopped him from claiming more victims from their tribe."

"Stopped him?" Ander said doubtfully.

"Yes stopped him, but at a great cost. Now a demonic being, it could not hunt for itself, but instead demanded blood and victims through other vampires."

"Considering what happened to your clothes, I take it you weren't planning on taking him down. What changed?"

Ema sat silent for a moment thinking how to answer his question. "You're right, however once he made a veiled threat against me, he made himself a target. There are certain laws that govern the metaphysical, and this is one of them."

Ander blinked. He looked less than certain for a moment. Then he said, "So that's it for Donny? How does something that's managed to live for over two hundred years get kryptonited by you?"

"Two things," She said in a quiet voice, "first, he promised a sacrifice from a family under my protection."

Then she added, "Donny fled New Orleans to escape from me, but I did not forget him. I knew that someday we would face each other, especially after what he did."

Ander nodded at her. Then, after a quiet moment, asked, "What did he do?"

"He made his brother Clemente into a vampire."

"I thought he killed him."

"No, before I retrieved his body from the monastery Donny stole it and made sure it transformed into a vampire; a dangerous one, much deadlier than him."

Ander frowned at her for a minute. Then he said, "How much worse can it be than something that feeds on human blood?"

"When something holy or good is turned to the purposes of Evil, its power is heightened. It can seduce the most incorruptible being. That is its danger. He hunts humans and other beings not only for their blood, but also for their goodness. I left New Orleans in pursuit of him, especially after he killed my pocket."

"Did you ever find him?"

Ema's eyes were intent, and serious when she said, "No, I never found him, however I guessed he made efforts to know of my whereabouts throughout the years."

"Why would he do that? I thought he would be afraid of you."

Ema turned to look at Ander, "Because he loved me."

"Loved you?"

"Do you remember when I told you his family forced him to take holy orders?"

"Yes."

"Clemente would never have chosen religious life voluntarily. He fell in love with me. I turned him away, but his obsession grew when I refused his advances. He even grew jealous of my avatar. He did not know the exact nature of our relationship, however he saw her as a rival for my affection."

Ander drove without saying another word, watching the darkness on the road disappear before the headlights. He looked back at her, and asked, "What happened, Ema?"

"Her name was Blanche Beaupre, a terceron and a free woman of color. She worked as a midwife, who would have met her end at the hands of a cuckolded husband. A captain of a ship came home to find his wife gave birth to a child that could not be his. He wanted no one to know of this shame, so he sent out thugs to murder Blanche the midwife who assisted at the birth."

Ander smiled slightly. "You saved her?"

Ema continued, "They sent Blanche a message for help in a birth late one night. They waited for her in an alley, stabbed her and left her for dead. She became my pocket for over twenty years. Clemente believed I trusted her implicitly, which I did, however he did not understand the nature of our relationship. She navigated the backstreets of New Orleans and heard of many dark rituals. Thanks to her, I brought many to purgatory in those years."

"What about her family?"

"Blanche became a bride in a left-hand marriage as a *placées* when she was very young. Her husband died, and their one child, a son was sent to France to study. He joined the military after he finished his education, and he never returned to New Orleans. Her other family died of old age, or the fever took them."

Ander arched an eyebrow. "So how did Clemente kill her?"

"Becoming a vampire did not lessen his love for me, or his hatred for her. Clemente stalked her and waited for an opportunity when he knew I could not help her. He slit her throat, and let her bleed to death, however he still did not understand my true nature."

"But he wrote La Dame Rouge on the back of your portrait."

"I believe he received missives from the Vatican to watch me, but again he did not understand their true interest in me. He attributed the title to the color of my hair."

"Were you sent by the Vatican, Ema?"

"A small group within the Vatican operated in secret, which is quite a feat for a place that is cloaked in secrecy to begin with. These cardinals were feared even by the Inquisition. They investigated the Figueroa family in Spain, and asked for my help in the New World. Many inhuman things fled to the

Americas with the flood of humanity that crossed the Atlantic. Trailing Don Ambrosio Figueroa became only one of several reasons I came to New Orleans."

Ander rubbed his face, and drove in silence for a few minutes before turning back to Ema. "You said Clemente follows you, why?"

"He wants to kill any sentient avatar that I have claimed. Clemente fears me, but this is outweighed by his desire to separate me from any human that I love."

"Would he kill me if he had a chance?"

"Yes. He already tried."

Ander swallowed and asked, "How?"

"Who do you think sent a vampire to take over the dog man that attacked you? He conspired with his brother, but has also witnessed Donny's destruction and let it happen."

"Do you think he'll try again?"

"Yes. Why do you think I have waited a hundred years to hunt with an avatar of your caliber?"

"Did Clemente kill your last special pocket?"

"No, but he did try once."

Ander looked across at Ema, and though he did not lead a dull life before meeting her, it paled in comparison to the secret world he discovered through her.

"Don't you think it's time we killed that son of a bitch?"

"Yes." She answered.

They drove in silence the rest of the way to Ander's home.

XXVII. If You Came Looking for Trouble

THEY WERE LESS THAN FIVE MILES FROM reaching their destination when a blue light flashed behind the truck. Ander eased onto the shoulder of the road, wondering why they were being stopped. In the truck's side mirror he saw the young officer who came to his house only a few days ago walking towards them.

The officer came to the window, and in a monotone voice asked Ander for identification. No flicker of recognition crossed his face. His skin was gray, and wet with a thin sheen of sweat.

In the same flat voice the officer asked, "Where is the woman?"

Alarm bells went off in Ander's brain. Without answering the question, he looked next to him and no one sat there.

"Officer what woman are you talking about?" Ander said in a calm voice.

The policeman shone his flashlight beam all around the interior, but only Ander squinted back at him.

"Please step out of the truck."

Ander opened the door and stepped out into the chill night air, but he did not close the door behind him. He stepped away, and stood listening to an all-pervading stillness that surrounded them. Somehow, the stretch of road became a lonely, eerie place.

A scurry of movement sounded in the darkness beyond the road's embankment, a rattle of pebbles and snapping twigs followed. The other man put his hand on his gun, and they both waited. Perhaps a deer lurked there, but Ander suspected something else hid out of sight. He thought of his pistol sitting in the center console of the truck.

A wind, cold and implacable blew through the inner chambers of Ander's brain. It did not come from outside his head. He would later recognize it as a heightened awareness of evil and danger, which came with being Ema's pocket.

They both waited for a long time. As if temporarily forgetting Ander, the officer returned to his car and paced the road near it. His hand rested on the door handle when an orange flare lit up the forest, and in a second, it went out. The void of stillness broke with the noise of animal life scurrying about, and something else too.

Ander surveyed the tree line expecting to see deer rush out, but then a sour stench of decay filled his nostrils. He felt rooted to the spot when he glimpsed several naked figures that ran out instead. One of them smashed into the side of the police cruiser, and for a moment, he stared at the expressionless eyes of a creature that could not be described as being quite human. They crossed the road and melted into the darkness of the woods, the sound of their movement becoming fainter. The fetid order trailed behind them.

An unexpected wind rustled stiff leaves, and Ander strained to hear any unnatural noise. The officer stood transfixed, like a robot that has been disconnected from a power source. Ander peered into the darkness, and something drew him to step beyond the edge of the road. Ema's cool hand touched his, "Do not go out there, no matter what happens! They are waiting for you." He thought of the things that crossed the road minutes before. A vague stirring in the underbrush displaced the silence. He felt them hunched in the gloominess beyond the pool of the vehicles' headlight. They were waiting.

In an instant, he recognized the rush of feet coming up behind him. He pivoted on the ball of his left foot, turned and struck the policeman with a straight punch to the face. The man's nose crunched under his fist. Ander couldn't understand why the officer tried to jump him.

The cop stepped back and circled around him, blood pouring from his nostrils. He rushed in, Ander drew back quickly and jabbed him in the solar plexus knocking the wind from him. As he stumbled back, he hit him once hard on the jaw and the man toppled back unconscious.

Ander stared down at the man, rubbing his knuckles that were skinned once again. They bled in some places where the scab had ripped off.

Exhilaration thrummed in his body because he could confront someone tangible. Coping with this situation placed him in well-known territory.

Ander looked at Ema who stood watching him. Her eyes gleamed in the semi-darkness. "Ander let's put him back in his car, and handcuff him to the steering wheel. He's being influenced; someone used him to make us stop here."

"I wondered why he acted as if we never met before."

"We have to hurry, out in the open we are easy targets, and I feel that something is building up."

With Ema's help, he carried the man back into his vehicle and left him there. Ander saw Ema freeze, and look around her. She told him in a whisper, "Turn off his vehicle, and run to the truck and turn it off as well. Now!"

They sprinted back to the truck, and he turned it off. Ema told him to turn off the headlights and not wait for the delay. He took out the pistol and clipped to his belt. Everything went quiet, except for the ticking of the engine as it cooled.

The ground shook, and they saw a disturbance in the forest as tall trees swayed making way for something passing through it.

"What has he done?" Ema asked herself.

A rustling in the bushes announced the arrival of the human-like creatures, which crossed the road earlier. They bolted around the truck with eyes that once expressionless, were now filled with terror. They had a look of something being hunted, and which found no place to hide.

"What are those?" he asked Ema, unable to tear his sight from the things that stood frozen in place trying to gauge which direction to run in.

"Those are Penitents." she said in a grim voice.

Ander looked at Ema with questioning eyes.

"They were once humans who fell in love with punishing themselves, and were seduced by their experience. They worshipped pain in place of the Divine. Their prayers were answered, and all they have found is madness and endless terror."

"What are they running from?"

"That!" Ema pointed to a figure emerging from the trees.

The creature towered at least ten feet in height, if not more. It was bipedal and as it stepped forward, Ander saw that the head appeared somewhat reptilian, but unmistakably interwoven with human features. It had a short snout, and only slits for nostrils. The eyes were placed in the front of the face like a man's, even though they glinted with a yellow light. The mouth ran wide across the jaw line below high cheekbones. Human ears, like small seashells hugged the sides of its head. Smooth scales covered its body in a mottled pattern, which lightened towards the belly and throat. It looked monochromatic in the moonlight. Muscular arms extended from its long torso, and the five fingers on its hand ended with sharp, black nails. The creature stood on long legs that tapered to elongated, clawed feet

Once it left the cover of the trees, they saw its short tail swished back and forth in a constant motion. It sniffed the breeze, and then pealed out a predator's cry.

Ander tore his eyes away from the reptilian creature that surveyed the road, and found Ema taking off all her clothing. She flicked the button for the sunroof, and in one swift movement, she catapulted outside of the truck and stood on its hood. However, she now stood clothed in skintight armor that rippled with colors as she moved. Blood red bled into maroon that melted into deep purple, then swirled with violet. Before his eyes, he saw her hair braid itself behind her head and a bright green Luna moth clung to the end of it.

She looked back down into where Ander sat, and dropped something that he caught on instinct. A long dagger, carved with an intricate design shone in the light from the dashboard.

"Its name is Iron Horse, keep it close. Do not leave the road, and beware Clemente."

The Penitents scattered in different directions as the beast bellowed again, studying the woman who stood there almost eye-to-eye without any fear.

The muffled sound of someone screaming intruded into Ander's consciousness. He looked out the back window of the truck, and saw the police officer yelling inside his car. Another reptilian circled his vehicle, entranced by the movement inside, but unable to find a way to capture it.

Ander sprang from the truck. He couldn't let another man be killed, by something that looked like the scientists at Jurassic Park cooked it up in their lab. He stuck the dagger in his belt, and pulled out his pistol watching what he called a "lizard man" turn its attention to him. It eyed him as if trying to determine in what direction he would run. Obviously, these creatures were not accustomed to being confronted. The cop looked at him with wide eyes, than back at the creature; all movement ceased inside the cruiser.

The beast let out a screech that ended in a bellow, and advanced on Ander with plodding steps. He saw it hunch it shoulders, tense its leg muscles and he recognized it planned to charge him. He drew out his pistol, and using the laser on it aimed for the chest. He pulled the trigger once, and he saw the animal stagger a bit, but only a small trickle of blood blossomed below its shoulder. It threw its head back, and roared with pain and fury.

The call echoed again from the other one, and he saw that it headed towards him as well. Ema sprang on its back as it stepped by her. She punched it twice in its ear, it fell to its knees and she sprang away from it as it reached around trying to tear her off its back.

In the few seconds that he saw this play out, he wondered why she didn't zap the thing into oblivion instead of punching it. His moment of questioning ended when the lizard man rushed him again, and he fired twice more. He saw that bullets only slowed it down. His eyes were drawn to the shotgun positioned in the front seat of the police car. If only he could get his hands on the riot gun.

Then like an answer to a prayer, the Penitents came running across the road again in the opposite direction like a herd of gazelle. Ander looked upwards and saw what caused them to flee. A bat-like thing with a man's face cleared the treetops than dove down, and landed in the middle of the road. He transformed into a tall figure, emaciated with a pale complexion. His dark, sunken eyes glittered with cool contempt.

Headlights cleaved the darkness behind it, and a small car playing loud music drove up on the scene. The driver hit the brakes, and four teenagers stared open-mouthed at the tableau. After a momentary silence, shouts erupted from the car, "Dude, back up!" and other invectives were hysterically shouted.

The vampire stood in the road and hissed at them with yellowed fangs. The lizard men followed with their own ear-splitting screech. Tires squealed as the car reversed, weaving across the road. It disappeared around a bend, and they heard it speed away.

Ema's voice rang out with an echoing tone, "Zeruko Neskamea." He looked towards her, and saw that she held a sword in her hand that glinted along its length in the moonlight. In a fluid movement, she ran towards the truck and jumped from its hood towards the reptilian. She came down using the pommel as a club, and hit it sharply on the top of its head. It crumpled under her, and lay still.

Ander saw that between him, and the shotgun stood a lizard man and a vampire. He realized without asking this was Clemente. Like Donny, his looks were dark and aristocratic.

Ema walked between Ander, and the otherworldly beings.

"My love." the vampire called out to her.

"Clemente, what have you done bringing these creatures into this dimension?"

"Are you upset with me after so many years without seeing each other?" The vampire grimaced in an imitation of a smile, its appearance changing as its ears elongated out from between its hair.

The lizard man screeched its call, and the vampire turned and hissed at it. He may have brought them to this place, but obviously, he did not control them. It charged the vampire, and Clemente swiped at it with claws that were curved and razor sharp. The creature howled in pain as deep gouges were carved across its chest. Blood burst forth, and ran in rivulets down its midsection.

Ema threw a disc of light at Clemente that sent him sprawling. With blinding speed she straddled the lizard man around its neck, and like its companion, she knocked it senseless with the pommel of her sword.

Suddenly, Ander felt a vise-like grip pull him back by the neck. The putrid odor of its breath filled his nostrils as it spoke to Ema. She advanced upon them, and Clemente stroked Ander's neck with the tip of a long fingernail. He angled it next to his jugular, which jumped with adrenaline and blood.

"Do not be so hasty, my lady. Haste makes waste, and do you want to waste his life?"

A wave of revulsion flowed through Ander but he could not break the vampire's grip.

Ema's eyes were dark and unreadable as she stared at Clemente. "I do not think you would be pleased, if you knew what I want."

"Well, then let's talk about what I want." The vampire laughed in hollow tones.

Ema remained silent.

"I want to be your companion, the way we used to be so long ago in New Orleans. I made two ill-fated mistakes. One, I should have heeded your warning about my brother, and the second has to do with your servant; I forget her name." He ended with a dismissive tone.

"Blanche." Ema stated in a quiet voice.

"Yes, Blanche. Perhaps I got a little carried away, but you must understand that for years I saw you share your secrets with her, trust her in a way you never did with me. Do you know how many times I went to confession, and asked for penitence because I wanted her dead?"

"Clemente, I never promised more than my friendship."

"True, but a heart sees hope in the smallest thing. I painted you so that I could look at you whenever I wanted. There are things that are sometimes beyond a man's control, and killing her became one of them, even though technically I could no longer be called a man."

"Blanche did not cheat you out of any type of relationship with me. It would have been the same between us without her presence."

The vampire's voice became more guttural as it spoke. "Let us not talk anymore of the past, but the future. If you want to spare this man's life, take me as your companion, otherwise I will kill him. I came close with the tall, blonde man, but this time I will not leave it in the hands of another. If you refuse me you will suffer, the same as I do."

Ema's voice grew hard as steel. "So there is no way to convince you? If you release him, because of what we once shared, I will let you leave."

"So that you can hunt me at another time?" the vampire asked in a purring, mocking voice.

"It is more than I have ever offered a creature like you."

Clemente's grip tightened around Ander's neck. "I see that the one who will not be convinced is you. Perhaps that is our destiny; to duel over humans. You love them, and I kill them. Perhaps one day you will tire of this, and accept me."

"Clemente, do you remember my names?"

"The ones the Vatican gave you? You know they were terribly frightened of you. La Dame Rouge, La Dama Roja; they spoke it only in whispers and then all conversation ceased. They were crawling out of their red cassocks, hunting for a hole to hide in."

"Are you forgetting one? La Dama de Sangre. The Lady of Blood." With a movement that blurred the eye, Ema pulled out the iron dagger hanging in Ander's belt, and plunged it into Clemente's heart. With her other hand, she pulled her avatar out of his reach.

The vampire issued a high-pitched scream that dwindled into a bellow. Clemente gasped, and tried to grab the dagger, but it burned his hands when he touched the pommel. He fell to the ground, the sizzle and smell of scorching flesh filling the air. Ema looked down at the vampire as it writhed at her feet. She knelt on one knee, and pushed the dagger deeper into its chest. "This is for Blanche."

A jet of burgundy blood spurted from his mouth, and he clutched again at the dagger. Black, bat-like wings erupted from his back, and wrapped themselves around his entire body as it curled into a fetal position.

Ander asked in a grim voice, "I know he was dead to begin with, but is he destroyed now?"

"No, only immobilized as long as the dagger is piercing him." Ema replied.

XXVIII. Somewhere in Time

EMA SEALED THE RIP INTO THE DIMENSION where the reptilians existed, leaving them on the other side. A dog man, one of the offspring of the one taken over by the vampire spirit, waited in a patient stance for Ema by the tree line. She went to it and asked for its help in rounding up the Penitents, and holding them on Ander's property until they arrived.

Ander went to the police officer who sat white-lipped in his cruiser. Dried blood caked his face from the broken nose. He flinched when Ander opened the car door. Ema walked up behind Ander, and stared at the officer. She reached out her forefinger and placed it on a spot between his eyebrows, and he went slack and fell backwards against the seat.

Ander with hands on his hips looked down at the prostrate man. "What do we do with him?"

"You know the dream sequence in movies?"

Ander nodded his head.

"We can't make him forget, but we'll make it seem like a dream. But we have to account for the time that he's been off the radio."

She took the Iron Horse dagger, and knocked him slightly on the back of the head in a spot that it would be impossible for it to be self-inflicted. She stepped back, and Ander took the handcuffs off.

Ema turned to Ander, "We must leave, because I don't think I can sustain the illusion much longer that's kept other vehicles from coming down this road."

Ander drove them to the house. Off in the east, the sky lightened. Ema grabbed something that emitted a muffled growl from the back seat of the pick-up. About the size of a football, it had a shriveled, human face surrounded by dark, scaly wings that enfolded it.

Ander followed Ema towards the back of the property. Under the gazebo, a dozen Penitents bleated like sheep while a black-furred dog man stood sentinel. Upon seeing Ema and Ander, it walked back into the woods and disappeared.

A tall figure detached itself from the umbra that covered the back entrance of the house. Despite all that he witnessed so far, Ander stumbled back a moment, looking at the broad shoulders of the jackal-headed figure that bowed to Ema. She handed him the Clemente thing, he then went to the gazebo and with the tip of his spear, opened a doorway outlined in blue. He escorted the Penitents to the opening, and then stepped through it. It closed in upon itself sending out a few flickering blue lights like fireflies that disappeared into the air.

"Ema, where is he taking them?"

"To redemption Ander, they are all human souls that deserve a chance to escape the torment of living in the grip of Evil."

"Even Clemente?"

"Yes, before his brother corrupted him, he was a man, imperfect, flawed, but he demonstrated kindness to the poor that came to him at the monastery."

"How long will they be in purgatory?"

Ema stared steadily at Ander. "I don't know. Their soul determines that, in a moment of perfect clarity where there is no deception about motives and total responsibility is accepted."

The first rays of the sun peeked over the horizon when Ema took her sword Zeruko Neskamea lovingly in one hand. The pink diamond glittered in the pommel of the Toledo steel sword. Centuries before, it had been forged by Spanish blacksmiths who recited prayers while they molded the white, hot metal into being. Along with the Iron Horse dagger, it disappeared into a red cube that already had claimed her armor.

Ema's shoulders drooped, as Ander opened the back door of the house. He swept her up in his arms, and her first instinct was to protest, but instead she laid her head on his shoulder.

He took her to the bedroom, laid her on the bed and drew the covers over her naked body. He lay next to her, and stroked her hair that held a scent of hyacinth.

He whispered more to himself than her, "I am remembering my beautiful Sibyllina that we have crossed paths before this lifetime, and you are not the only one that knows how to watch over those they love."

www.ingramcontent.com/pod-product-compliance
Lightning Source LLC
Chambersburg PA
CBHW031318170626
46807CB00002B/475